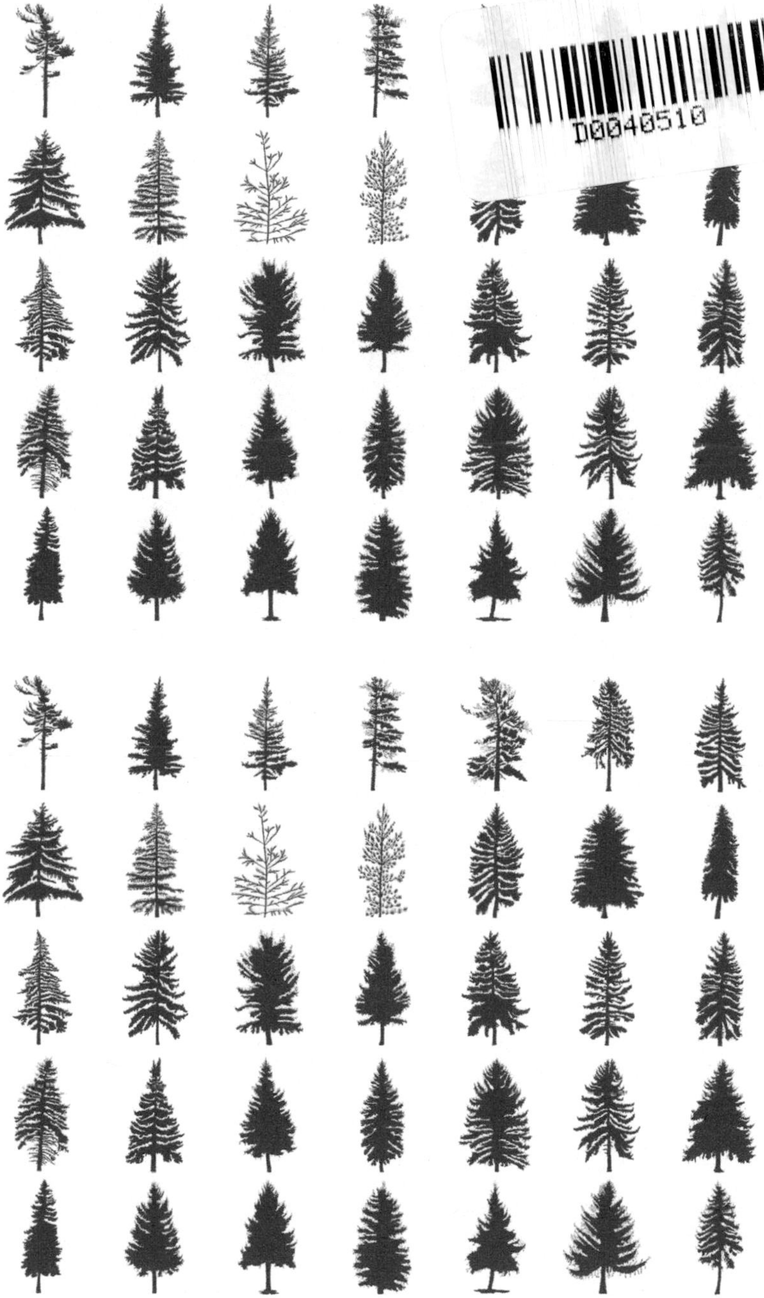

The Tree In The Town Square

And other short stories

Sam Calvo

First Paperback Edition. Press.

www.samcalvo.com | sam@samcalvo.com

ISBN (paperback): 978-1-7358735-2-7
ISBN (ebook): 978-1-7358735-3-4

Disclaimer: The events and conversations in this book have been set down to the best of the author's ability, although some individuals' names and details have been changed to preserve their anonymity.

For anyone who feels the same

The Girl In The Blue Beanie

The first time I decided to drink at a bar by myself was when an unusual heat wave swept through the small waterfront neighborhood, parching the sidewalks that had been dampened from the recent rainfall and crowding the beaches with locals who had never seen the metallic strips of their thermostat jump into triple digits. Like many others, I was kept inside my apartment for longer than I would have wanted. With all the blinds drawn over my windows and surrounded by fans, I was shrouded in a heavy and steamy darkness with occasional light that crept through the window blinds, painting the carpet in thin bright stripes. Everyone I knew had fled town to avoid the heat so I was alone for the next few days. Alone may not be the most appropriate word as the city bustled with many others who would have to brace the irregular weather conditions. Uncomfortable may be a better word. While one could easily go outside and meet others, my irrational desire for isolation kept me away from the crowded beaches—and the fear of developing a coping dependency on spirits kept me out of the bars. Instead, I decided to find companionship online.

The prospects today had dwindled as if there had just been a mass exodus. I assumed many, like my friends, had fled town to avoid the heat. I had been sending messages for hours with no response until a girl wearing a blue beanie laying on a concrete floor came across my screen with four words written on her profile:

Want me? Insult me.

Pleasant and monotonous conversations plagued my prior dates. Talk of one's place of work or the town they grew up in or whether they prefer cats or dogs was mostly what was spoken about. These topics were safe and they placated the possibility of any unwanted hostility. And it wasn't healthy. I knew this all too well because when they spoke about such things I tended not to listen. But it has become a crutch. And in front of me, this woman with honey blonde hair and warm beige skin laying on a concrete floor wearing a bright blue beanie was a possibility for something else. But it wouldn't be as easy to relinquish this crutch as I thought. I sent her a benign message.

Do you think you can handle getting insulted by me?

I discarded my phone to the other end of my couch and turned on the TV. A man with a deep, cavernous voice

3

wearing a white chef's coat was squeezing a molasses-colored goo onto a spinning cake. Then, only after a few moments, my phone chimed. I reached across the couch for it and to my surprise, the girl in the blue beanie responded.

Of course I can. But in that photo of you eating a burrito, it looks like you're thinking about why your mom doesn't love you.

I looked at the photo on my profile: me eating a burrito at two in the morning in the backseat of a car after possibly half a dozen drinks. My eyes were bloodshot but my teeth were flashing. She made me grin and I sent a message back.

I'm eating a burrito at three in the morning, of course my mom doesn't love me.

She had to respond to that, I told myself, and I anxiously waited, repeatedly turning my phone on and off. The space around me felt like it had slowed down. The rush, and excitement, and the will to do anything felt . . .

cumbersome . . . long . . . dreadful. I gave up and retreated to sucking on a nearby joint . . . which felt nice on the lips. For the next few hours, I wore a complacent, church-going smile . . . and the bright streaks of light faded from the carpet. The nightfall, however, did not stop the heat from melting the gum on the sidewalk or dehydrating the plants on my balcony, but it was late enough for me to drift . . . into a dizzy . . . intoxicating sleep; one that felt empty . . . without a response from the girl in a blue beanie.

//

A virtual business meeting, an early one that accommodated workers living on the east coast, was slated right when my alarm went off. I rubbed what felt like breadcrumbs out of my eyes and sat at my desk. Before the meeting started, I checked my phone and saw that she had not responded. My bank, however, notified me that I had an upcoming credit card payment of $535.24. Then, the tiled videos of my co-workers started multiplying on my computer screen like a cracked wasps nest and the meeting officially started.

One department suggested streamlining our current manufacturing process with robust automation tools that could help employees efficiently meet their performance goals. However, another department expressed hesitation in this process and warned about over-automation. They feared that replacing the roles of certain groups of employees would be a workplace shock and could hurt morale. The meeting ended with the realization that a different department was needed on the call for clarification, so another meeting was slated for tomorrow morning.

I stepped away from my computer and made myself a bowl of cereal. The blinds still covered all my windows to keep the heat out, so I sat on the couch with my phone and ate my cereal in the darkness. Even with the blinds drawn, the couch was hot and sticky and my skin stuck to it like chewing gum. The girl in the blue beanie had not responded and I felt pitiful. I discarded my cereal bowl in the sink to let it join all the other dirty dishes. They could be friends, I decided. The space around me had slowed down. The weather outside was piercingly hot . . . and minimal movement felt like the only way to keep cool . . . I got up and laid on the floor. Within minutes, my back started to feel achy . . . so achy . . . I took an anti-inflammatory with lukewarm water. I decided . . . after a bit of thought . . . to stand up. I realized that I had not counted the protruding knobs on the drywall . . . next to my refrigerator . . . so I did that. I counted . . . one hundred and thirty-six knobs. Eighteen minutes later, I went outside and watered my dead plants. It was hot . . . yes. The heat created a sort of blanket . . . a heavy blanket . . . that everyone had to wear if they wanted to be outside, but heavy blanket or not . . . I'd still be more inclined . . . to tend to my protruding knobs . . . as well as all the activities in my apartment I had at my disposal.

I watched a TV show about cakes and played solitaire on my coffee table. I ate leftover tandoori chicken with tortellini salad . . . which tasted very good . . . and very pleasant in my mouth . . . and read three pages of a book by Albert Camus. I set up my amp, fiddled with the tuners, and strummed three strings of my electric guitar . . . then I discarded it in the corner of my living room. I thought about counting more protruding knobs . . . so much more to count . . . but I wanted to do something mildly productive . . . so I put my dirty clothes in the washing machine, which had been sitting on the counter for two weeks now. I decided to take care of two errands today. One was to pick up . . . a package of joints from a nearby dispensary . . . the other was to buy peanut butter and jelly at the grocery store . . . I wanted to make sandwiches. Both trips took a combined thirty-eight minutes, and in no time, I was back on my couch . . . hazy-headed . . . with a smoking stick sitting in a small ashtray . . . and a peanut butter and jelly sandwich eaten to the crust.

I inadvertently took a long nap and was unaware of how long I was out. The air around me felt heavy, tortuous, and the small drops of peanut butter stuck hard to the plate like they were glued on. I propped myself up and reached for my phone across the couch. The girl in the blue beanie responded.

I don't think that's the only reason your mom doesn't love you. Also, are you allergic to peanuts or good haircuts? Because I can't tell.

She made me smirk in a way I found hard to describe. It was in the way that made me forget the way I think. I immediately wrote back.

If I'm allergic to good haircuts, then you must be deathly allergic to good fashion taste.

Then the waiting resumed, but it did not last long. Twenty minutes later as I was trying to read more of my book, she sent a message back.

At least I know common phrases . . . what the fuck is 'fashion taste'?

I decided against finishing the chapter I was on and messaged her back.

Well, I assumed you knew English, so let me explain. It's related to your taste in fashion.

She didn't hesitate this time. Our conversation must have spurred her interest because she immediately wrote back.

I just don't think anyone caught dead in a straw hat should be lecturing anyone on fashion

On my profile, there was a photo of me at the summit of a mountain in some national forest I don't remember. I wore a straw hat that I had purchased in Oaxaca a few years prior. It was a cute insult, so I decided to look at her profile. One photo was of her standing in front of the mirror at the gym, flexing her bicep. I wrote back to her.

Am I really taking this shit from someone who takes post-gym bathroom selfies?

I sent it with a smirk and from there, we had a texting cadence. While I was moving my washed clothes into the dryer, she replied.

At least I'm hot enough to take gym selfies. You look like you haven't been in months. I'd watch out for gusts of wind if I were you.

I had been thin all of my life, and that was true. I responded back.

Last time I checked, having a personality and a sense of humor has more longevity than your biceps.

On her profile, I saw another photo of her. She was wearing a black suit with lingerie underneath and cheetah print heels. Her blonde hair was wrapped in a high ponytail and her face was coated in makeup. I added more.

Also, I don't think dressing up like a sub-par escort gives you any more authority than me on giving fashion advice.

She replied as I was folding my bedsheets.

Not an escort. I was at a party with friends . . . sorry, I didn't know you don't know what that's like! I just assumed everyone has friends. My bad.

And that's when I asked her out to dinner, but she did not reply, so I resumed my anxious waiting. I routinely checked my phone until the hours went by and the premonition that she would not respond settled in my head. I didn't receive any messages from anyone the rest of the day, but at least my bedsheets and laundry were done. Productivity could be a distraction from my unease, so I drove to the gym. When I got there, I had no energy to even lift the lightest dumbbell, so I ordered a strawberry smoothie from the nutrition cafe next door and drank it on the drive home.

The darkness had fully taken hold of my apartment now. The daylight that had crept inside in the form of those bright streaks had faded. The darkness didn't knock, ask politely to come in, and sit respectfully in a guest chair. It simply made itself home because it knew it was home.

Everything had slowed down again and I wasn't sure why. I re-watered my dead plants and counted the protruding knobs on the drywall in my closet . . . two hundred and nineteen, more than the last time I counted . . . which made me think that I had overcounted or did not do a proper job of keeping count in my head. Then . . . the couch sucked me in. I laid down with my back slouched and my feet propped up on the ottoman. I took another anti-inflammatory . . . I felt ripples of pain . . . and lit my joint, a combination I had no interest in knowing whether benign or fatal. I sent her a follow-up message before I fell asleep to a TV show about cakes.

//

The next morning I rubbed the breadcrumbs out of my eyes and before anything else, I checked my phone, but she had not responded. I got out of bed wearing the same heather grey shirt as yesterday and joined the meeting about yesterday's meeting. The meeting had the needed department, but they did not give the insight the other departments were looking for. They did, however, recommend a different department that could give them the answers they were looking for. Another meeting was scheduled for the following Monday—including that department.

I stepped away from my computer screen and made myself a bowl of cereal. The blinds were still drawn and the darkness had enveloped most of my apartment with faint streaks of light poking through. I peeked outside through the blinds and felt the warmth of the sun on my face. My thermostat registered triple digits and all impulses in my body tugged at my brain to stay inside. And what a lovely day it was to stay inside and live in the slowness that had enveloped me.

I made myself a peanut butter and jelly sandwich . . . and watched a video about the nuclear disaster at Chernobyl. When I was watering my dead plants . . . I was surprised to see . . . that a red and white flower . . . on one of my balsam peppermint sticks had wilted. It was now overtaken . . . by a hideous dark shade of brown. It used to be beautiful, I concluded . . . so I gave it extra water.

I went back inside, looked over at my pile of unfolded laundry, and sat on the couch. I couldn't find the remote, so I tried reading more of my book . . . and I kept reading . . . until my eyes felt . . . heavy. The remote was wedged in between the couch cushions, so I set my book aside . . . and put on a TV show about cakes. The burnt herbal and woody smell was still pungent . . . I cracked open a window, letting in the hot air, and I reached for my joint and blew the smoke outside after each suck. My mind went hazy and the cakes looked more . . . delectable than ever. I searched on my phone for nearby places to pick one up. The grocery store would do, or I could drive to the main market street to get an assortment of . . . cupcakes, which I rationalized as just smaller, cup-sized versions of cake. I continued searching until the decision paralysis set in. I discarded my phone to the other end of the couch and kept watching TV. Then, it buzzed and with impatient giddiness, I reached for it and saw a new message from the girl in the blue beanie.

A double text deserved that extra wait time. Also,
what makes you think you can handle me in person?

She always made me smirk in sort of a cheeky way. I
thought about if I could handle this in person or if I actually
wanted this in person. I wrote back.

I think I can because I know you're probably not this
clever in real life. I'm more concerned whether you can
handle me in person. And I don't think you can.

And then we had dinner reservations that night at
Asadero, a Mexican restaurant I suggested for its proximity
to the main market street. We got a table for seven o'clock,
which came slower than I thought. I tried to pass the time, so
I counted more protruding knobs and watched more TV
shows about cake. Asadero was ten minutes away, but I left
my apartment at six-thirty. I usually don't like to drive when
I'm feeling this way due to the almost unwavering impulse I
have to veer off the road and drive straight into a lamp post,
so I walked and made it to the restaurant before she did. The
heat was somewhat forgiving in the evening, and with extra

hydration and parts of the walk shaded by trees, my sweat stains weren't noticeable. I had planned for this as well, applying the stick of travel-sized deodorant under my armpits.

I waited outside until she arrived five minutes later, wearing jean shorts and a white tank top. I gave a childish smile as she got out of her car and walked up to me. She had the piercing blue eyes of a gemstone that almost seemed to glitter as she got closer. When we were finally face to face, a brief silence fell between us. She overapplied her perfume, I thought. A luscious scent of sandalwood and Moroccan jasmine permeated the air around her. She scanned me up and down. "I'm happy to see you wore your best outfit for me."

The humidity stripped me down to a pair of shorts and a graphic t-shirt I got from a gift shop in Vancouver. I looked at her outfit again. "I know you're an escort and all, but maybe next time you can actually try to dress up."

She raised an eyebrow. "You're lucky I'm even here. Looking at your outfit, there's no chance in hell you could afford me."

And then we found ourselves inside, sitting across from each other with two glasses of water and silverware. A

Spanish song with maracas played softly over the speakers nestled in the corner. She grimaced at me.

"So what do you do besides wear awful clothes? Your profile said you work with computers."

"To an extent, yes," I told her. "It's a job that requires a brain. A functioning one I might add."

We spoke in a dull, monotone manner as if we had known each other for many years and could know what each of us meant without the inflection in our voice.

"That's very cute," she said, twirling a strand of her hair not in a flirtatious way but in a necessary way as if she was untangling a knot. "What's it like being a virgin?"

"What's it like fucking anything with a pulse?"

"Better than being a virgin. At least I get the opportunity to feel the warmth of another person."

"Is this why you spend so much time at the gym? Just so someone will find you hot enough?"

"Big talk for a man who has probably never experienced anything truly wet. The computers don't help, but your clothes and mommy issues are probably why."

I gave a curled smile and took a swig of my water. "And what do you do besides take vanity photos at the gym?"

17

"I'm a nurse. So, you know, I actually help people instead of typing nonsense on a keyboard."

"Oh, like a doctor but not really a doctor? Did you give up halfway through your medical track and settle with being a glorified assistant?"

"Nope," she stated contently. "Just took happiness over money. Something I can tell you probably have neither of."

Before I could respond, the waitress approached the table to take our order. We both scanned our laminated menus.

"Can I get the Sonora torta?" I asked. I had butchered the Spanish and the waitress let out a soft giggle. "But without the Anaheim peppers and beans?"

"Oh," she blurted out while still studying her menu. "He's also a picky eater, and he doesn't eat spicy foods?"

I raised an eyebrow at her. "Is there a problem?"

"No problem at all," she said with a smirk. "It's just . . . I usually don't go out on dates with pussies."

I glowered at her and she returned a quick but cheeky smile, all while looking at her menu. Her eyes moved around, scanning each item with much intention until she seemed content with a decision.

"Well, since I actually care about what I put in my body, can I have the prime ensalada with spring mix, cotija cheese, and cherry tomatoes please?"

I scoffed. "You might as well eat out of a lawn mower bag."

She darted her eyes at me. "You might as well die at sixty from heart disease."

"At least I have a heart to actually die from heart disease."

"At least I won't die from virgin pussy disease. Your body seems to be riddled with it."

The bartender gawked at us for a moment, probably wondering how two people could possibly talk to each other with such vitriol. She hastily grabbed our laminated menus and left. She only came by twice after that: to bring our food and our bill as quickly as possible.

"I don't even know why I'm here," she said, shaking her head. The swan white pearls hanging from her earlobes jiggled. "You probably piss despair and bleed mediocrity."

"Those are big words from someone who went to a college with an eight-five percent acceptance rate."

"And it would have slipped a quarter of a percent if you had applied."

"I wouldn't even think of applying to a place with such a rigorous and selective admission process."

"You're right. They're probably at quota for virgin pussies."

"Virgin pussy seems like your type of guy."

"So you're openly admitting that about yourself?"

"Nope. Just stating an observation."

"I observed that you order food like a toddler."

"I observed that you order food preferable to rabbits. You know, If you still have room for dessert, I have some plants back at my place you can nibble on."

She gave a curled smile. "That's assuming I'd even want to go back to your place."

And then I found myself back at my place with her on top of me. Her blue beanie flung somewhere around the room and her blonde hair still knotted in a high ponytail. My bedroom was covered in darkness and my bed was surrounded by a circle of whirring fans. The heat inside was so humid and thick you could cut a hole through it. But we didn't care. Bubbles of sweat dripped off her chin and onto my shirt and my back puddled the sheet with a sticky liquid. The scent of sandalwood and Moroccan jasmine was overtaken by our stench, which smelled of used rags and old cabbages.

"You fuck like a paraplegic," she said in between breaths.

"Sounds like your normal clientele."

"My normal clientele makes twenty times what you probably make. That's how they can even afford something as amazing as this."

"I thought you knew I wasn't enjoying this."

She took her ponytail out of a knot and flung her hair over her shoulders. "Of course you are. You should feel lucky your dad's condom broke so you can be here to enjoy this."

And after a few more minutes with a dint of persistence, we were both putting our clothes on. We did not speak to each other until we were fully clothed. I gave her a glass of water with ice cubes and a cold towel. She had taken out her earrings and asked me to hold on to them for her while she put on her clothes. I stuffed them in my pocket so I wouldn't lose them.

"If you're going to have a wardrobe of shitty clothes," she said while standing in front of one of the oscillating fans, "you should at least fold them." She pointed

21

to my unfolded laundry on top of the dryer. I gave her a tense look but didn't respond, as I knew the extra warmth in my room would soon be sucked away. And we did not speak to each other for a time while she gathered her belongings. The only sound in the apartment was the whirring of the fans and the occasional car that drove by outside. She seemed pleasantly comfortable with the silence while I had knotted my insides over it. She had driven both of us from the restaurant, so I walked her to her car parked around the corner.

"Hey," I said to her as we stood in front of her car. My voice trembled but was filled with the most sincerity I could muster. "I actually had a really good time tonight. You know . . . I think you're really sweet . . . and funny . . . and I'd like to see you again."

She gave me a blank face. One a squirrel might give if it saw oncoming headlights. She looked down at my pants. "I hope you weren't planning on stealing my earrings."

"Oh, right." I padded my pants pockets and pulled out the swan white pearls and placed them in her hand, which were warm to the touch. She got in her car and drove off, and the flickering neon sign across the street was beckoning for me to step inside and let my worries spill out like the squeezing of a molasses-colored goo onto a spinning cake. I walked across the street and filled my defective container with the fermented malt liquid that came from the cold opening of the bottle clutched in my hand. And instead of spilling out and exposing their hideous shape, the worries remained burrowed inside of me, content and happy, and they danced among themselves to a harmonic melody that sounded quite familiar.

The Milk Bottle Under The Bed

I hit another roadblock in my writing so I called my grandparents. I had just finished a manuscript over the course of several months but I found the story appalling and deemed it unfixable, so I started again with a blank page and a blank story and a blank meaning, all of which needed to be filled.

I called my grandmother, Noni, and asked her if I could bring over some lunch. I usually spoke with Noni when it came to making plans. Papo, my grandfather, had a difficult time with that, among many other things. She gleefully accepted.

We decided on sandwiches and I would pick her up and drive us to the nearby market. They lived in a single-floor condo on the lake since stairs became too troublesome and their home in Palm Desert had become too long of a trip for them to take.

"You know he can't go to the desert anymore," Noni lamented about Papo as we drove to the market. "He thinks he can, but he can't. Some days he looks good and others not so good."

"Yeah," I agreed. "He looked well at my mom's place a while ago."

"You know he wants to do the things he used to do."
Noni sighed and shook her head. "He wants to go out and talk to everyone, but he can't anymore. He just can't"

And this was miserably true. When we spent time together, Papo would talk to everyone we interacted with. Waitresses, baristas, grocery clerks, anyone with a mouth, really. He loved everyone and he saw something in each of them. In Palm Springs, he would play eighteen holes of golf in the morning with friends and meet us at the country club grill over scrambled eggs and sausage links. He was always surrounded by people, always talking or jeering or laughing with them. I think he misses that deeply.

Papo was also very frail. He used a walker to get around and spent most of his time at home. His diabetes was unforgiving and no doubt stripped him of the many things he loved. "I wouldn't wish this on my worst enemy," he would say to me when injecting his insulin. Noni was also noticeably frail as I had her hold onto my arm to walk up a few steps to get into the grocery store, but was still more mobile than Papo. We picked up three sandwiches from the market and went back home where Papo was sitting in the recliner watching a World War II documentary. Noni put his sandwich on the kitchen counter.

"They didn't have deviled eggs on rye," she said to him. "so we got you a tomato and basil."

Papo, without saying anything, gave a soft smile and carefully got up from the recliner. With trembling hands, he picked up his sandwich off the counter and sat outside on the balcony. Noni and I joined him after pouring ourselves and Papo a glass of water. We sat around a glass table in flimsy chairs with cushions patterned in flowers. They were the same chairs I used to sit in when I was a child when they lived back near Lake Hills. It was in a small cul-de-sac and when my mom brought me to visit, I would spend most of my time in the basement where Papo had an old pinball and slot machine.

And the reminiscent thoughts flurried around in my head, dancing to a harmonic tune that I could not hear but only assume was playing for them, but this was when my mind would become disgustingly self-aware and eventually devour itself. I thought about our sandwiches and how many more I would be able to eat in the future. I had thousands, even tens of thousands of more I could eat in my life while they maybe had a few dozen or so. And to think of how morbid life becomes if you measure it by anything insignificant. If tomorrow, a doctor told Papo that he would only have six months left, he would have, while blunt but true, twelve more farmer's markets to attend, six more bills to pay his internet provider, and one more dentist appointment. Noni would have two more haircuts and one more oil change if given the same news.

We all sat on the balcony, enjoying our sandwiches.

"Noni, did you go to high school here?" I asked.

She nodded. "I went to Franklin then we moved to the south end of Seattle by the Kline Galland home."

Papo held up his sandwich to Noni like it was a box of tissues. "You want some of my sandwich, Rachel?" he asked in between mouthfuls.

She smiled and patted his arm. "No thank you, sweetie."

Papo slowly nodded his head, as if there was a rusty spring in the back of his neck, and continued eating.

"Anyway," Noni said to me, "the area got really bad and our kids were in fifth, sixth grade. Then a bunch of kids from their school, five of them, got them when they were riding their bikes. And they were new bikes! They started harassing our kids, and they knew them because they went to the same school. So I said that's it!"

"When you get older you can't eat like you used to!" Papo blurted out. He placed the uneaten half of his sandwich back on the plate and pushed it away. His head slumped over like the sinking head of a sunflower at the end of summer. I felt he was trying to keep up with me. His appetite had been taken from him.

"I know," I told him. "I have a tiny stomach and I probably won't finish my sandwich either. It's alright if you save it for later."

Papo lifted his head and looked around the deck in a way that made me think he was seeing the view for the first time.

"I bought this place," he said to nobody.

"Yes, you did," Noni warmly said, patting his varicose hands.

"You know what made it?" he said. "You pay cash. That's the only reason."

"What happened?" I asked.

"Well," Noni said. "Three times we tried to buy the place, and each time the lady said no. And finally she sold it to a doctor, but he didn't qualify."

"He must've had awful credit," I joked.

"What did you say?" Papo asked Noni in a jarring way as if he had been abruptly woken up from a nap.

Noni kindly rolled her eyes and turned to him. "I said the lady who bought the house said the doctor did not qualify."

"Oh. Right!" he assured himself. Then, he turned to me with widened eyes. "Could you imagine?"

"I don't believe it."

"So I told Papo, 'I don't care if you pay more, we're going to buy this house!' And the real estate lady told him, 'Don't show it to your wife!' "

"Hm'what?" Papo abruptly asked.

"I said the real estate lady said to not show it to your wife."

"Oh."

"And I told her, 'I know what the place is!' and we tried to get it three times and we wanted to find the key and—"

"How's your place down there?" Papo interrupted.

Noni raised an eyebrow. "Excuse you."

I smiled. "I love it. Marvelous. Very quiet."

"Good," Papo said.

"He's got a nice place," Noni mentioned.

"I still use my record player," I added.

"Mmmm, very nice!"

"Whatizit?" Papo asked.

"He uses his record player," Noni said to him. "Remember he has this old record player at his place?"

"Oh."

Noni rolled her eyes and smiled at me. "Where'd you get it again? You said somewhere special."

"A vintage shop in Fremont. Old vintage shop. Have tons of things from the fifties and sixties, and someone brought in a record player."

"I wish I would have known. I had a bunch of records I would have given to you."

Papo lifted up the uneaten half of his sandwich in the air, displaying it like a foreign object a child would find on the ground. "I can't eat it," he announced to us.

"Don't worry about it!" Noni told him. "No one's pushin' ya."

"How's the sandwich?" I asked him.

"Very good," Papo said, debating whether he should take another bite. "Can't eat it all."

"Don't matter," I told him. "Doesn't matter."

He put the sandwich back on the plate and looked over at the lake, watching the cyclists zoom by on the street. He looked placid now, in a sort of way where he now understood that this lake was familiar.

"You both went to high school together?" I asked Noni.

"We graduated from Garfield," she said, wiping a smudge of pesto that was dotted on the side of her lip. "He was a year ahead of me. And my mother wanted to move to Seward Park because we were living on 26th Avenue. Not the greatest place in the world. We grew up with everyone. We grew up with blacks and whites and Asians and everything, and we didn't think about blacks and whites and whatever it is, they were just neighbors. We just didn't think of that."

"So how old were you two when you got married?"

"That's a good question," Noni said, tapping the table with her fingers. "Umm. I was about . . ."

"Yo'bratha was in the army," Papo cut in.

"Who?"

"Your *bratha*."

"Oh. How old were we when we got married?"

"Who?"

"We."

"*We*? I was-twenty-two!"

Noni chuckled and turned back to me. "I think we were twenty, twenty-two."

Papo blurted out. "Dummy!" he said, smacking his forehead with his palm.

We all laughed. Papo got up to go use the bathroom. He grabbed his walker and took gingerly steps inside. They were slow, mechanical steps like ones you'd see on a toy you would wind up from the back.

"And it was tight," Noni added. "We had three kids in like four, five years. Two years between each of 'em. So it was difficult. And I wasn't educated." Then, gesturing to Papo who was inside, "He wasn't educated."

I realized that I did not know if they went to college. How I could have not known this fact was beyond me. They must have told me before and I had not listened, or I was young and probably distracted by some new toy or video game. I wanted to preserve this fact now. It would be good to know.

"Neither of you went to college?" I asked.

"No," Noni shook her head. "My father wanted me to go to college, so I went for one semester, but if you're dating somebody who's not in school, it doesn't work."

"What was Papo doing?"

"He was out of school. He was working at that time with his dad at a produce company."

"Out of high school?"

"Yes, out of high school. He got out of school every day at two-thirty instead of three o'clock and helped his dad. And he had a vegetable place where you sell vegetables. Helped him bring the boxes, lift crates. That's why he was so strong. Had very strong shoulders. So we were fourteen, fifteen, and dating in high school. And the only time we didn't date was when he pissed me off when he was supposed to come and pick me up and he was late or didn't show up. I told my dad, 'I don't want to see him. I'm not going with him!' Then he says, 'Rachel, he's sitting here.' And he was just there on our couch waiting for me. I said to my dad, 'I don't care, send him home!'"

We both laughed.

"I remember you told me that he took you to a very nice Italian restaurant for your first date," I said.

Noni smiled and reclined in her chair, squeaking the rusty springs underneath. "He did! He picks the best thing on the menu and tells me 'this is really good!' And now usually the girls wait for the boys to say, 'Oh, I'm gonna get an ice cream or have a float,' or you know. He didn't say that. He said 'Oh, the cutlets here are very good.' So I said, 'Okay I'll get it then.' And they were delicious. But he didn't order it. He got south pie and ice cream because he had no money."

"Wait, what was it called? South pie?"

"Apple pie."

"Oh, you said south pie."

"Oh, no, no. Apple pie."

I nodded. "Ah, okay."

"So we were going home. And about ten blocks away was this library. Still there, I think. We get to the library, and it's pouring down rain. He says, 'You know, it's kinda nice. It's refreshing.' And I didn't know nothing, I was stupid, so he says, 'Let's walk home,' so we walked in the pouring rain because he had no money. We couldn't take a cab or drive. He didn't drive until he was seventeen or older, I think. And we lived right next to each other on 26th Avenue, so we got to the house and both of our dads were on the porch waiting for us. They were so worried."

Papo took cautious steps back onto the balcony as if his body weighed him down and sat in his chair. The chair rocked and squeaked as he made himself comfortable.

"What?" he blurted.

"I was telling him about how we walked home from Yesler Library," Noni said to him.

"Oh."

Noni started laughing. "He says he has no money!"

"I had no money," Papo said to me as if he just had a realization about this.

"Well how the hell would I know? Never ask a girl what they want if you're not expecting—"

"Sam!" Papo blurted out. "Raining like hell."

We all laughed.

"And is your back okay?" Noni asked me.

"Yeah, it's getting better. I got cleared to play basketball, but I still have some pain here and there, so I just have to monitor it and gauge—"

"Sam!" Papo blurted out. "Do you need anything?"

I chuckled. "I don't need anything."

"Don't say that, you'll get me mad!"

"I don't need anything! But eventually, I'll want to go on vacation."

"Oh, very nice!" Noni said.

"Call me before you go," Papo said.

"I will. Absolutely. I'll bring you something back."

"Just bring yourself back," he said. He turned over to Noni and smiled. "You know," he said to Noni, "I'm like his grandma. *My grandma*! Jeez, my grandma. You know what she used to do? She used to give me money. *Twenty-five cents*!" he said, shaking his hand out. "I went crazy. She used to give me a quarter and I would go to the Madrona theater and see a show. Costed you twenty-five cents."

"It was a lot in that time," Noni added.

"That's crazy to me," I said.

"We'd go a lot and it—"

"You what?" Papo interrupted.

Noni turned to him. "We'd go to the movies,"

"Oh," he said, shaking his head. "No popcorn. I loved popcorn, but no popcorn. It costed fifteen cents. A drink was ten cents. And what's really good was candy. They gave you big candy bars for ten cents." Papo extended his hands out to show the size of the candy bar, about the size of a folded leaflet.

"What was your favorite?"

"Nuggets, I think they're called. Chocolate nuggets."

"What movie would you go see with twenty-five cents?"

"Whatever was playing," Noni joked.

"Hopalong Cassidy," Papo said. "Roy Rogers. And then sometimes, it was twenty-five cents for my mother and father. They would sometimes go to the shows. I remember I was working and all of a sudden this guy, I didn't know who he was, he wanted apples, so I gave him apples. He grabbed the apples and ran! Next door was a fire and he was a fireman, and he had to go there."

"He used to work very hard there," Noni mentioned.

"Yo'what?"

"Your father. He worked morning and night."

"And when my dad saw Rachel," Papo said to me, "he used to give her two pounds of cherries! She would sit down on the curb and eat them and eat them. I'm surprised she didn't get sick!"

Noni laughed and rubbed Papo's hand on the table which was, like hers, frail and riddled with veins. A tender gesture. "I loved cherries!" she exclaimed. "And my mother used to go shopping there, and so he would see me there and

38

give me cherries. I just sat on the curb and ate them. I was so happy!"

"Every Friday and Saturday we used to go to the wholesaler and buy apples, oranges, and produce. Things like that. Then my dad would buy me breakfast. 'What do you want?' the waitress would ask him. My dad said, 'Standard.' That was just two pancakes. Orange juice? *No.* Too much money. We had just two pancakes. No orange juice."

"How much would it be for just two pancakes?" I asked.

"Ooh, I really don't remember," Papo said, shaking his head in a way that told me he didn't want to remember. "But nobody had money,"

"And we didn't have the education," Noni added. "We didn't have too much."

"My Bar Mitzvah," Papo said. "I got a watch from my father. I wanted a bicycle because I didn't have one. Was too much money. He bought me a watch."

"We didn't have the money at the time."

"You know what linoleum is?" Papo asked me.

I shook my head. I truly didn't know.

"It's a floor," Noni said. "Not a tile floor or anything, just plain linoleum."

"It's called linoleum," Papo stated. "Everybody had it in their house. My dad underneath used to put money. Money? I said. What for? For vacation."

"At the time you didn't trust the banks, and so if you wanted to go on vacation you had to have the cash." And as if it had just occurred to her, she turned to Papo and said, "You know all those things you know, I don't remember it being bad times."

"Bad times? No," Papo asserted. "No shooting. You left the door unlocked. It was quiet. Now you have to have a submachine gun!"

We all laughed. The lines around their faces scrunched together. Noni's eyes looked warm and refreshed. Papo flashed misaligned and yellow teeth.

"And if you met someone," Noni added, "you shake hands, and if they wanted to borrow some money or something they'd pay it."

"Seems like a nice form of neighborly trust," I noted.

Noni nodded. "Mhm, I'd say so too."

"And your parents came from Turkey, right?"

"Yes, my parents came from Turkey and so did Bill's."

"And your families didn't know each other until you moved?"

"Hmmm," she turned to Papo. "Bill, how did our parents become neighbors?"

"Huh?"

"You know if your parents met my parents before being neighbors?"

"I don't know," he said, deflated. "I don't know."

"Well, because—"

"But they saw your dad and they didn't like him."

Me and Noni chuckled.

"So if they came from Turkey," I asked, "where did they stop first?"

"Only my dad came from Turkey," Papo said to me. "My mother was born in Spo- no, Portland. Portland?"

"So did they stop in New York?"

"Yes, for immigration," Noni stated.

"And then how did he travel to Seattle?"

"My dad's brother was here," Papo explained. "He tells him, 'Come here. It's just like Turkey. We have water, food, and lakes.' And he was talking about Alki Point. Then

I had my dad's mother, my grandmother lived upstairs from us." Papo shook his head and gave a melancholic look. "Jesus, It was terrible."

"And she used to wear the black hat and everything," Noni added.

"I used to sleep upstairs with my sister," Papo said. "In the old house we were born. All of a sudden, I got to pee and I'm not going downstairs! So you know what I did? I took a milk bottle under the bed and peed into it."

"Well, they were steep stairs!" Noni remarked. "And they were hard to go on because we were kids."

"That's just what we did . . . That's just what we did." And there was a long pause until Papo said, "I think they weren't that bad days. They were nice days. It was nice days. I have no regrets growing up. We had nothing. Nobody had nothin'. We'd watch Hopalong Cassidy, Gene Autry. They were nice days."

And it was a nice day if I had allowed myself to believe so. Shortly after, I said my goodbyes and left. Noni gave me a squeezing hug and Papo told me to be careful and to enjoy my life. After I got into my car, I pulled out my phone and saved the audio recording. And as I was about to replay the track to make sure it was clear, I looked up at the sky, an azure blue painted with strings of clouds, and decided in my head that it was not a nice day.

The Lemon Tea Without Taste

I have a friend who's studying for business school
I have a friend who's never had a thought that was truly his
own

I have a friend who recently got married
I have a friend who I hold no envy towards

I have a friend who hates meetings
I have a friend who cries at the smell of burnt wood

I have a friend who brings joy everywhere he goes
I have a friend who became what I feared most

I have a friend who I met my first day of college
I have a friend who said my writing was awful, sloppy

I have a friend who was raised by parents who couldn't hear
him
I have a friend who attentively listens to everyone he meets

I have a friend who I don't think is my friend anymore
I have a friend who—

And I lifted my fingers from the keyboard and reclined in my chair. My eyes started to strain, so I pushed myself away from the screen. And away from my screen, and any other screens, seemed like the right decision.

I put a record on the player, but the music didn't come out. I took a sip of my lemon tea, but it had no taste. Another dreary night was illuminated by a faint lightbulb in the corner of my apartment struggling to stay lit while I tried to avoid the purple passages like pastries in a display case. Why say anything insightful when your only purpose is to sound insightful? Why weigh yourself down like a ball and chain? Why come to an absurdist understanding of the world when you feel like you cannot do anything about it?

"You're pretending again," a voice from behind said. I turned around and He stood by the kitchen sink with a cup of lemon tea, which he took a sip from. "This tastes like shit. And it came all the way from England."

"It used to taste good," I timidly said.

"*Used* to. Now it doesn't," He asserted. "It tastes like shit."

"I guess."

He took another sip, made a disgusted face, and spit it into the sink. "Is this the part where you try to sound deep and profound? You want to capture the human zeitgeist?"

"I'm more concerned with capturing myself."

He walked over to me and delicately played with my hair; twirling a few strands together and gently pulling them out of my scalp.

"How can you write about such things when your life has been fully encapsulated in excesses of freedom and comfort and pleasure?" He said as he played with my hair like a monkey eating lice off another.

The dim light flickered in the corner and I slumped my shoulders down.

"I don't know."

He knotted a few strands together and plucked them out. It felt like a pinprick on my scalp—a familiar pinprick. "How vain it is for you to sit down to write when you have not stood up to live?" He released my hair and pointed to a few things around my apartment: a heartfelt birthday letter from my parents, the refrigerator in my kitchen, and the sixty-five inch television in my spacious living room "This is not living. This is the life of a lonely king, given everything

47

without resilience and who is already dead by the time the crown is placed on his head."

I cowardly hung my head down and He gave me a contemptuous look.

"You are blessed to have these thoughts. A starving child in Nigeria will never get to have these thoughts because his stomach will not permit it."

He leaned against the desk, eyeing a few discarded sticky notes and crumpling them up.

"I need to take a shower," I said.

He shook his head, unsurprised, with a crumpled sticky note in his hand. "This is the third time today. Your skin is going to end up feeling like sandpaper."

"I need to think," I reassured Him. "My eyes hurt."

He spoke very sharply now. "How about you leave your room? You can't think of anything when you're trapped inside of here."

"I like it here."

"You like to believe that."

And as I was surrounded by the ceramic-tiled walls of my shower, I yelled for Him to leave and I was left surrounded by a cloud of steam and the remaining echo of my shout. I dried myself with the towel hanging over the curtain and returned to my desk. I wiped the loose hairs off my desk. They delicately fell to the floor, twisted and curled for me to see. My physical anguish was peeling at me like an onion. The screen was still so demanding of me, daunting if I thought about it long enough, so I retreated to my couch and watched a movie.

The next day while at an evening picnic with friends sitting around a cooler of hard seltzers and a wooden board coated with different crackers and cheeses, I realized that I was smiling hard. Not grinning. I'm the saddest when I have a huge grin on my face, but this time I was smiling. All my teeth were showing. One of the girls in the group started to share a story.

"So we planned on hiking Shelcaster Lake that morning and camping at the summit," she said to the group, "but when I picked up Whitney, she didn't have a backpacking tent. She had one of those spacious camping tents that weighed like twenty pounds!"

Everyone laughed.

"What a stupid fucking story," He said, sitting next to me. He was flicking small pebbles off the ground with his index and thumb.

"I think it's pretty funny," I said to Him.

"Are you serious? Wasn't funny or even clever. Just a dumb water-cooler story. You used to have a sense of humor."

"So we get to the trail," she continued, "and we strap up this *super* heavy tent to her backpack and like she's so small that the tent is like pulling her down to the ground!"

Another roar of laughter.

"Ha. Ha. So funny," He said.

"Will you shut up?"

"How can you even enjoy this? Such tepid and contrived drivel, it's like they're programmed to speak."

"I'm trying to."

"I don't know why you are. You should just go home. Just go home and be by yourself. You don't even need to be here. The conversation will still go on without you."

"I'm trying to enjoy myself."

"Do you think they're enjoying you?"

"I'm trying to enjoy myself."

He scoffed and started pulling clumps of grass from the ground. I took a sip of my seltzer but could only feel the liquid going over my tongue.

"So what did you do?" one of the guys asked the girl.

"We just said, 'Screw it. Let's book a room at a resort!'"

Another roar of laughter. I was also laughing.

"And so we get to the resort, right," she continued. "And we show up with all of our backpacking gear looking like we were lost in the woods for days. Totally out of place. And the concierge takes a quick look at us and says, 'You all must've traveled far to get here.'"

A few giggles rise from the group. A small band was playing music on the other side of the park. I saw a man slapping a steel drum and two women strumming oddly shaped guitars, but I couldn't hear them.

"How have you not blown your fucking brains out by now?" He asked, holding a giant clump of dirt and grass in his hand. "Are you ready to leave yet?"

"I'm enjoying myself," I told Him.

"I thought you said you were *trying*," He mocked.

I ignored the snide remark and returned my attention to the group. A conversation was had about interviews and hiring new people. One girl in the group, who had moved from Ohio, was ready to leave school to find a job but was dreading the interview process. Another was groaning about how awful some candidates were in the interview; not dressing appropriately, failing a situational test, not writing a proper thank you letter, but kindly offered to give the girl in school a referral to his company.

"All this is very juicy," He whispered to me. "You could write about how people are so in love with their own enslavement that they'll even put the shackles on their friends."

"Will you shut up?" I butted back to Him.

"That this entire establishment of corporatized life envelopes you in a life of solitude devoid of any meaning and fulfillment so you would do anything to get any sense of release. Even making your friends suffer with you."

"That's not the point."

"You really mean that?" the girl from Ohio gleefully said to the man who had offered his referral. "That would mean so much. I don't know how to thank you."

"You should thank him for helping you imprison yourself," He said to me. I ignored him and took a sip from my seltzer that touted a strawberry taste on the label, but I tasted nothing.

"Of course," the man said to her. "Just send me an updated resume and a cover letter so I can get you in our system."

"So bring a record of your suffering and a letter stating why you want to suffer more?" He said to me again.

"That's great!" the girl from Ohio gleefully said. "I really don't know how I could thank you."

"No need to thank me," the man said. "I'm just happy to help."

"And there goes her life," He said to me again. "Maybe you can make her a main character in some dystopian novel. You know, make her this person that loves the bureaucracy of systems and order and obedience, but she can slowly turn to hate it all. To see the ugliness in everything. You know? Something like that. And you can make harsh critiques of capitalistic wage labor and unfettered consumerism and you can envelope the entire narrative—"

I held my palms over my ears and angrily whispered incoherent nonsense to Him until my body felt weightless, like a feather that could be carried away and dropped into the nearby lake if a gust of wind rolled through. Get the earwig out of your head. It has burrowed itself so deep. Everything around me looked so flimsy, like it could all be carried with me in that same gust of wind and we would fall in the ocean and drown together. I tried to re-enter myself in the conversation but the words spoken out of everyone's mouths became twisted and their faces were grainy. I closed my eyes and shook my head, and then in an instant, the feeling melted away, and I was flung back into a conversation about renting a boat for a weekend party.

And in a jagged interval of the conversation, I announced that I had to head home. With a quick look, they didn't look at all taken back, but I glanced away before I could register anything else. I took apart the camping chair I was sitting in and collected the snacks and drinks that I had brought with me in a small bag. I slipped my shoes back on and walked on the cement path toward the parking lot when a glass bottle slipped through a hole in the bag and shattered on the ground. I looked over and He stood next to me and just smiled.

"This was a great foraging day."

//

The work week had gone by in a sort of slow, mundane haze. Meetings were scheduled. Projects were completed. My breakfast was the same and my head hit the pillow without any thoughts about the uniqueness of the day that had just happened. During the week, the melancholy dripped from my body as if I had just walked through a rainstorm; the perfect weather conditions for writing, I thought to myself. I had not written or seen anyone in five days, and the mental calendar that hung from a thumbtack in my head reminded me that I had given myself a deadline that was approaching.

I had nothing to write about this morning. My desk stained with grey wood was lopsided on the right side and wobbled if you put enough weight on it. A dull yellow pencil sat alone in a black circular container next to a few crumpled sticky notes. Then, I started to write.

Watering your plants and forgetting to eat breakfast

Curing yourself by not taking a single pill

Eating a burger while looking at a chart of the Global Hunger Index

A copy of Architecture Digest discarded in front of a homeless encampment

The company Veracity Financial Group charged with financial malfeasance

A video about the atrocities at Treblinka interrupted by an advertisement for a buffalo chicken sandwich

Walking through a botanical garden of songbirds while listening to a podcast

"I can't imagine you're serious now, are you?" a voice from behind said. I turned around and He was standing in the kitchen with a cup of lemon tea. He took a sip and spit it back into the sink. "Still tastes like shit."

I ignored him and went back to typing on my keyboard. He hated it when I ignored him, so he walked over to my screen and grinned hard.

"You should call your grandparents."

I didn't look at him. "I already saw them."

"You could get more."

"I don't need more."

Then in a sinister tone, "You could always have more," he hissed.

"That's not the point," I told Him. "That's never the point."

He scoffed and backed off. My cell phone buzzed with a message from a friend asking if I wanted to watch the fireworks for the upcoming holiday.

"There's nothing for you there," He chimed in, flicking his hand as if to swat away a buzzing fly. "There's nothing for you to use."

"It sounds fun."

"You'll get there and hate everything and want to go home."

And I knew He was only saying that because it had happened before. He had no way of knowing that it would happen again, but something inside of me was telling me it would.

"It's a good reason to get outside," I noted. He grimaced back to me.

"But you like being here."

"I don't like being here."

He smirked. "Then why are you here? You're always here and nowhere else. You want to be here. You *like* being here."

I shook my head. "I shouldn't be locked up here for this long. It's not healthy."

"You never cared about your health," He pointed out.

I was fit, in shape. I regularly exercised and ate good food, but He already knew that.

"Not that kind of health," He said. "You know the kind I'm talking about."

I got stubborn, ignored his comment and walked past Him to the kitchen. I opened a cabinet above the sink and pulled out a box of lemon tea bags.

"You're avoiding me," He said, raising his voice. "You know what I'm saying is true. You just don't want to accept it."

"You don't know what's good for me," I snapped. I scrunched my nose as I fiddled with the tea bag, trying to remove it from the plastic package.

"I know what you truly want," he said in a menacing tone. "I know what you truly desire."

My fingers felt wet and slippery like they were coated in some slimy goo. The package resisted my slippery fingers tearing at the perforated line. He came up to me and put a icy hand on my shoulder. I didn't like when He got too close, and he was extremely close to me.

"Go outside and hate everything," He hissed in my ear. "Or go outside and use everything. Doesn't matter either way. They both end up in hate anyways."

I muttered *shut up* under my breath, still trying to remove the plastic. He smirked and took his cold hand off me. My fingers went numb and I felt like I was opening the package with a pair of sticks. The sense of touch went numb. My body felt like it could collapse at any moment, like I was made of some sort of structureless jelly. He was still in the corner of my eye. I started screaming in my head, begging for it to open for me. Pleading for relief. *Please open,* I mumbled to myself. *Please, please, please for the love of God, open and have a good taste.*

"Why have tea when you can't even taste it?" He jeered, now leaning up against the kitchen counter with crossed arms. My fingers gave out and I threw the package on the counter. *Shut up*, I muttered louder under my breath. I furiously opened cabinets and drawers, looking for a pair of scissors. *Do not be weak*, I encouraged myself. *Do not show anyone that you are weak.* But I am weak. And I knew He was beckoning for me to sit back down and let the weakness unravel. To let my body become a perpetual, structureless jelly, and to live frail, feeble and without thought like a sedated dog.

"You hate everything," He barked. "You hate everything!"

I was now begging for Him to shut up under my breath, but he was right. I hate everything He says and does and feels. I hate it all. I thought about connecting my fist to His jaw, but that didn't solve anything last time, and I didn't think it would now. I slammed cabinet doors and shelves back. The hatred was boiling over me and I could feel hot steam collecting in my ears. I closed the last drawer with intense force, chipping off some wood from the side of it, and grabbed a steak knife. I stabbed the plastic package on the counter and ripped it open. I placed the packet in my teacup and He turned red hot.

"You hate everything!" He shouted. "You hate everything! You hate everything! *You hate everything*!"

I whipped my head around and screamed with every muscle in my body.

"SHUT UP!"

The room fell silent. And I had screamed myself into a void, leaving me with a shattered teacup on the ground.

This was not a time for me to be here, I thought, so I grabbed some few things and put them into a small knapsack. I closed the blinds and turned off the lights. I walked past the spinning vinyl on the record player and out through the door, making sure I was the only one who was leaving.

//

I drove east toward one of the largest national parks in the state, then hiked four miles up to a small forest that opened to the north shore of a lake. I hiked through mud and slippery rocks covered by small streams of water and a few wooden bridges were built over the larger rivers for easy access. Where the bridges weren't built, I forded through a few shallow creeks that wet the soles of my shoes. I childishly hopped and splashed the water everywhere like I used to on the stormy winter days. I would wear rain boots patterned with my favorite animal and would stomp around the drain line that ran along the end of our driveway.

Halfway up, my left ankle rolled to the side and shot a tight pain up my leg. I sat on a tree stump and massaged it before continuing up the trail. The sun was unforgiving by the afternoon. I was in such a rush earlier that I had forgotten to bring my hat, but thankfully, the sheltering forest of hemlock and cedar trees shaded my skin from the harsh summer sun. But I purposely left everything else in the car and only carried a small water bottle and a few granola bars. My pulsating ankle shouted at me with each step, reminding me that I should have brought some pills.

The ascent took less than two hours and the shaded forest eventually opened up to the lake, which was calm and translucent enough to see small groups of freshwater trout swim between the rocks and driftwood. I sat on a fallen log suspended over the edge of the lake where wildflowers had grown and gently dipped myself ankle deep into the cold, translucent water. A few curious trout swam up against my feet, thinking I was some strange new fish until they decided otherwise and fled away like flies dodging an incoming swat. On the other side, a small waterfall was emptying itself into the dazzling lake. A beautiful landscape, I thought to myself. One would only have a few good weeks to see the lake like this when it wasn't frozen over or being hit with a torrent of rain.

A few hours had passed as I took it all in. My body had relaxed and was not bothered by the protruding knobs of wood on the log poking into my thighs. Birds chirped from the trees and a woody scent permeated the air. My ankle also felt relieved of pain. It was too cold to actually swim, so I closed my mind and envisioned myself floating in the lake. My fingers made little ripples on the surface of the water, and a small piece of driftwood coated in colored bugs floated past me. Eventually, my body drifted toward the waterfall until my head was submerged under it. I opened my mouth and let the water fill in. I let my body feel what it would feel like.

And as I sat there on that fallen log, letting myself be away from myself, I had gently massaged my mind into a lucid nap where I felt, smelled, and saw everything. After what felt like hours, my body had brought only my available sensations back to me. My feet shivered from being submerged in the freezing water and my thighs felt sore from the protruding knobs. I took my feet out of the water and dried them in the baking sun. The skin on my nose also felt the heat as it started to peel and a small group of fish had returned to swimming around where my feet were.

After drying my feet, I put on my shoes and walked on a dirt path along the water's edge through bushes and tree branches, which I occasionally pushed out of the way. A small bird had scampered through some bushes, tweeting and fluttering its wings. I looked up at the mountains, their peaks snow capped and their bases covered in a precarious scree. If you squinted long enough and had an eye of what to look for, you could see patches of flowering glacier lilies sprouting from the melting snow. I never squinted harder. I found a clearing of bushes on the edge of the lake with a view of the descending waterfall. I saw the small fish again, swarming around a piece of driftwood in the translucent water.

Across the lake, another man, shirtless and wearing a straw hat, was flicking his fingers on a wooden kalimba, playing a beautiful melody. It was harmonic and tranquil, just like the lake. We made eye contact and he eventually walked around the lake toward me. We had a pleasant conversation. He even offered me a sip of his fermented tea drink, which tasted of an acidic pineapple with a garnish of basil. It was a pleasant taste. He then hiked down the mountain.

I grabbed a nearby stick, long and covered in moss, which I plucked off, and started drawing shapes in the dirt. A few triangles and squares along with my name written in cursive. I reminisced about my time at the beach when I was young. When that was exactly, I was unsure of, but I was holding a pail bucket of wet sand and a thin twig. My sandcastle was one clumpy mound of wet sand and I had drawn lines in front of it with my twig, acting like levees that would protect my little castle from the approaching tide. I remember feeling the wet sand between my fingers, soft and squishy like a therapeutic stress ball. I remember feeling the inevitable tide, which draped over the sand and coated my feet, carrying strings of seaweed that wrapped around my ankles. I remember the sun bearing down on my skin and the back of my neck starting to burn. I remember my mother calling me to play with the other kids who had come with us on the trip. I don't remember saying anything back. And all these feelings did not overload me in any way. In fact, I was the farthest away from any sort of sensory overload. It was rather, a perfect harmonic balance of feeling and appreciation. The fondness I experienced for everything around me and how they felt to me.

And this harmonic balance that I had not felt in a long time was slowly coming together now as I sat by the edge of the lake that was so ever translucent and pristine and beautiful. I felt I could shed a tear. Then, I looked over the lake and saw something peculiar. A single leaf, discolored and curled at the tips, floated in the middle of the lake. And

65

it stayed in the middle. A few gentle ripples of water made from the waterfall pouring in from the other side delicately nudged the leaf, but never moved it so much out of place that it would wash up on the edge with the driftwood.

The leaf can never escape, I thought. The leaf cannot leave the lake, no matter how tranquil and serene it may seem. The leaf will never know what it would feel like not to be in the lake unless a heavy gust of wind carries it away. But for the leaf itself, whether it decides to leave or not, will not have the ability to do so. It simply floats forever until it dies. And how I too float in this seemingly calm and tranquil lake of certainty. To keep myself the farthest away from the edge and gently pull towards the middle where the water has no waves or ripples. To not even know what it would be like to brush myself against the edge or even leave the lake completely and feel the hard and rocky dirt. And I looked over the waterfall, filling the lake and making sure it would never run dry. The floating logs of driftwood: merely distracting toys for me to play with. I'll never leave the lake because of how calm, how serene it is. And I would never need to know or want to know what any other sensation might feel like because it could be worse than what I feel right now, or better, but I wouldn't know if I could get it. *We'll never leave the lake.*

And something else had taken over me. I gathered myself and hiked back down the mountain in a hurry. I pranced over mounds of rocks and hopped over puddles of wet dirt. I ran through the streams of water, wetting my shins and ankles. My left ankle cried out in pain with each step I took, but I ignored the pulsating ripple. I bolted down the trail. "*We'll never leave the lake*," I repeated in my head. "*We'll never leave the lake. We'll never leave the lake.*" And then after a few dozen times, I said to myself, "*I'll never leave the lake.*"

I descended down the mountain and found my car at the bottom. I was now muttering to myself in a thick glob of sweat. "*The waterfall keeps pouring in*," I murmured. "*We cannot leave because we don't have the ability to do so. Yes . . . that's it. That feeling. Yes! We need something to help us leave. We are all leaves that cannot leave. We need the wind. A storm. A wave. We need something. We cannot do it ourselves. We cannot do any of it ourselves.*"

I kept muttering to myself on the drive back. The granola bar I brought was good, which I devoured while keeping a hand on the wheel. I drove in silence, not thinking once about putting on the radio. My mind was preoccupied with a torrent of thoughts. I had sped on the highway and passed slower moving cars. I drove past the salmon hatchery I had wanted to stop on the way back and ignored my body's urge to use the bathroom.

When I got home, quickly and frantically, I fiddled with my keys and finally stuck one in the doorknob and opened myself to the dark hallway. I flipped on the lights and entered the kitchen. I looked down and sighed. I grabbed a broom from the closet and swept the jagged ceramic pieces into a dustbin. I looked over at the stove and realized that I hadn't even boiled the water. I set a kettle on one of the burners and opened the tea bag package with a pair of scissors that was covered by a stack of mail. When the kettle whistled, I made my tea and sat at my desk.

Then, I started writing. And my body felt nothing. All my sensations rippled on my fingertips. And I wrote and wrote and wrote until my exuberance flickered out like a dying lightbulb, and I was overtaken with a somber feeling of regret. I had plunged myself back into a familiar feeling. And these walls that already felt inescapable had towered even higher. The familiar feeling filled my head, knowing that I had left something so beautiful without a true understanding or appreciation. It was a utility. And nothing more.

I glanced over at the record player, the stylus tracing the inner ring of the spinning vinyl. I flipped the vinyl over and played the back side, but the music would not come out. I let the record play for those who could hear it. I sat back down at my desk and took a sip of my tasteless lemon tea. Then my chest started thumping like a bass drum. My head clouded in a haze. The realization of my own self-indulgence threw me into a fit of hysteria. I covered my ears with my palms begging for it to stop. I felt a presence from behind me, but all my intuition was telling me to face forward. And I had felt this presence before, a familiar presence that I did not want to talk to. I turned around. Slowly. And He was standing in the kitchen, leaning up against the counter, with a cup of lemon tea in his hand. And as I gazed into his eyes, cockroach brown like mine, I understood that we were conjoined, destined to be a part of each other. Two inseparable pieces that would need to coexist. To the betterment or the detriment of the other.

I was trapped. And he knew it. And He looked into my dismayed eyes and gave me a crude smile.

"This was a great foraging day."

The Pizza From Piero's

"I don't know how to start this. I feel like I should be sobbing, that there's this unspoken but understood threshold that one has to meet to make this kind of call?"

There was a brief silence before the operator on the other line responded.

"It's most definitely not the protocol," she assured me. "What's more important is talking about what you're feeling. So, tell me what you're feeling."

"I just feel . . . awful."

"Well, you're not alone. Many people feel like this and I'm glad you decided to call today. Have you had thoughts of—?"

"I have. But so does everybody else at some point when the weight of it all becomes too unbearable. I'm not unique with these thoughts, and I think it's foolish for anyone to deny that they haven't had them."

"I see. But you're the one on the call so let's talk about you. Have you attempted—"

"If we're talking physically, no. Definitely not. If we're talking mentally, emotionally, psychologically, then this call may be a bit too late."

"But you're still here. And that's what's important. Do you have anything in your house that you could use to—?"

"Of course I do. I have steak knives, a hammer, a bottle of Aspirin. I live on the third floor, so I can just leap off the balcony and splat on the sidewalk. I also have these plants; they're Japanese plum yews, and apparently they're toxic, so if I eat enough of it, that'll probably do the job. There are harmful things everywhere. It just depends on whether I want to go or not. Wrap me into a straitjacket and toss me in a room with cushioned floors and walls, and I'll figure out a way if I'm determined enough."

Outside my bedroom window, a firework crackled in the distance followed by a group of cheers.

"It must be hard having these thoughts on a day like this," she said. "Do you know why you feel this way?"

Her tone was a bit mechanical as if she was reading off a sheet of paper with a list of acceptable responses, and understandably so. I'm not the only person she has talked to today. I reminded myself that I'm a number, a very large number. I stayed silent, long enough for another firework to sputter outside. I should have gone out. I should have made plans. I should have mustered the interest to leave my room.

But I didn't. Instead, I decided to lay in bed for hours—my mattress soft and plush—so much so that my spine fell out of alignment and my lower back rippled with a dull pain. But despite the mechanical tone, I found comfort in knowing that I would never have to meet her and that she would never have to meet me, and I became more apt to divulge my life to her.

"I—I feel like this," I said with a trembling tone, "because I have a terrible capacity for being able to live."

"And why do you feel that way?"

"I cannot enjoy many things and it drives me to insanity."

"That sounds quite difficult."

"It is," I noted to her. "I hate what a lot of people do and say and feel and think. I can be at a dinner table and find myself dissecting every sentence, every phrase, giving every word a scrutinizing sort of autopsy and looking inside, knowing I'll hate it all."

"Why do you hate it all?"

"Because I don't find the meaning in it."

"And how do you think that has affected you?"

My back flared up, so I tossed around until I found a comfortable position to put the pain in submission.

"It makes life lonely," I moaned. "I have an unrequited impulse to analyze every word that comes out of someone's mouth. I think about the tepid and apathetic things that are talked about while at the same time, I hold the delusional belief that I am somehow superior."

"Did something like this happen today?"

"It happens all the time."

"So what do you like? What do you like to talk about?"

"I know what I *don't* like. I don't like humid air, carnivals, dance circles, ice breakers, horoscopes, expensive spirits—"

"I think it's more important," the operator interrupted with a stern tone, "if we talked about the things you *actually* like."

"Okay. I like writing. I think I like writing."

"What do you like about writing?"

"It's an outlet for me to express myself."

"Do you think you're a good writer?"

"That's not for me to decide, nor would I ever decide that for myself. My mind will always balance on a tightrope between literary genius and pompous idiot, and I don't think I'll ever know which one I truly am."

"So why not join a local writer's group? You could meet other like-minded people like yourself."

"Writing itself is a solitary art form," I explained to her. "And I don't like going out of my way to meet people. It takes an enormous amount of energy, and I know I will inevitably grow to dislike everything they say."

"Do you ever leave your house?"

"I believe a writer is akin to a modern day forager: going out into the world to only bring back the necessary material to use for their next great story. To me as a writer, going out and looking for meaning is especially exacerbated because you look at everything that's happening in your life, in front of you, and you try to derive some great story or epic or metaphor or archetype. But the other day I was infuriated with myself. On one particular foraging day when I returned home and transcribed my experiences, I hated it all. I hated it all so much. And it wasn't that the writing was bad or that I didn't believe what I was saying or that I had forgotten to record something. It was only after I wrote the story that I realized I could not recall a single thing from that afternoon. I could not remember what street they grew up on, or even the names of the films they had seen when they were younger. I could not remember what kind of sandwich I ate, or even what they wore that day. A part of my mind had concluded that it was insignificant, and the reel in my head that would usually spotlight those parts of the day had stopped spinning. It usually stops spinning . . . it usually does that."

"And how did that make you feel?" she asked in a more sympathetic but still robotic tone.

"That experience I had was tarnished. And I know I only have a finite amount of them left. I don't know why I keep doing this to myself."

"Do you have a hard time enjoying yourself?"

"I remember an outing with some friends a few weeks ago. We were out camping at a remote beach, hours away from the city we lived in, and out in the ocean were these large rocks that looked like miniature islands. One of my friends asked if we would willingly live on one of these islands in a house for three years with all of our basic needs like food and clothing taken care of, but we could not leave. We would have the only house on the island, but our friends could visit. Many said they would. They thought it would be quiet and relaxing. One of them said that it would be a great writing retreat, then lightly nudged me. Solitude could uncover untapped creativity like a newly found oil reservoir and spur the creation of works I could never have imagined writing."

"It sounds nice. So what was your answer?"

"I didn't say anything."

"You didn't answer?"

"I didn't have to. The question was addressed to the group. Not just to me."

"But you had an answer in your head."

"I had two, actually. And not answers, reasons. The first, which I would have said out loud if it would not have punctured the pleasant atmosphere of the conversation, is that you are asking me to trap myself in a room while my grandparents slowly decayed and eventually died. And in my head, I allowed them to respond by asserting that they could visit and I would tell them, which was true, that my grandparents had to exert a herculean amount of energy to even leave their house, let alone travel many hours to a remote island. It would not permit them to visit, and they would die and there would be a burial and a ceremony while I was marooned on an island. The second reason, which I never intended on saying out loud, is that my writing is a sickness. And this sickness cannot be cured with isolation. In fact, I believe it is exacerbated with prolonged loneliness. And I know I'm not the only writer who feels this way."

And I noticed the words coming out of my mouth felt cogent and properly structured like I was reading a speech, as I could finally speak some of the thoughts that have hardened in my mind. I knew I had given her a lot, more than what she was probably expecting from this call. And I had so much more to give. There was a brief silence before she gave an understanding hum.

"Why do you think writing is a sickness?" she asked.

"First, I want to clarify that my comment about my grandparents is not rooted in altruism. It's about if given any fun and low stakes hypothetical, I go to the extreme and cannot play by suspending the dark reality around me. While I can respond in a fun and leisurely way, in my head, in my sick tormented mind, is an answer much more sinister than the one that escaped my lips. Second, it's not the writing itself that's the sickness—it's what I write about. And I avoid writing anything lifeless and against my own self at the expense of fame or wealth or notoriety. I write what I think needs to be written. I write what I think is truth. But I can also do the opposite. I can so easily do the opposite. I can write to make money by living on vapid aphorisms I know will be eaten up by others looking for meaning. I can tell the imperfect that nobody is perfect and I can tell the failed that failure will lead to success. And as I live in my luxurious villa too large for any one person to possess with all my riches too much for one person to spend, only then will I begin to understand my own decadence and the eternal truth that I had contributed nothing to the world that could not be replicated."

"Hmm," she said. "But we didn't get into why you have a hard time enjoying yourself?"

"It's because I'm selfish in the way I impose myself onto the world. Part of my suffering and pain from writing is that I need to look at every single thing and have to draw some sort of meaning from it. It has to make sense, or else it's worthless."

"So you need to find meaning?"

"Everyone does. Everyone has this insatiable desire to derive meaning from every experience we have. And it's very uncomfortable to not know what that meaning is. Sometimes it robs us of the holistic experience itself. And we all have this desire, to find the meaning in whatever we're looking at—"

"But you're the one on the call, so let's try and talk about you."

And it felt easy to talk about me to someone who took it upon themselves, to take a job that involved carrying the burden of others' sorrows. I would not burden anyone else. I will always try to prioritize other's happiness over mine.

Another firework sputtered outside followed by cheering. I wondered how much longer I would have to hear them, but if I was with them, I would not have that worry.

"Right," I said to her. "I cannot find my solitude and peace to write because of my inability to experience the world without the influence of my pure egoism. That everything in the world is happening to me. And if I could somehow puncture this attribute about myself, maybe I can find that solitude and peace."

"How would you go about doing that?"

There was a brief silence.

"Well . . . I called today."

"I don't think that would resolve anything."

"But it's inevitable."

"And you don't have to make that choice."

"You always make that choice. You will only die if you allow yourself to. Either your body will let you go or your mind will."

Her tone became a bit more comforting. "It sounds like writing is the cause of a lot of your dark thoughts."

"It may and it may not."

"So why do you keep writing?"

"Why do I keep writing?"

"Yes."

There was a brief silence before I decided to speak. I wanted to gather my thoughts and really say what I felt. How troublesome it can be to think of something for so long without ever saying it. I swallowed hard and took a deep breath.

"I write because too often I feel like I can't speak. Like my mouth is riddled with canker sores. Because this is the only medium where I can say the things I would never dare confide in anyone. It's where my unfettered mind can gallop along the vast landscape of pages. Some people get put in wooden boxes and buried under the soil with a headstone inscribed with only the information anyone will really remember them by without truly knowing their deepest thoughts."

And then I thought about whether I would know anyone's deepest thoughts about me, or is that reserved for later? For when the ramifications are so far removed that they would feel obliged to say these things. And I feared that the truest things anyone will say about me would be when I am buried too deep in the ground to hear them.

"And not everyone has to be a writer for their mind to spill," I told the operator. "They just have to be brave enough to let it."

"But we're here to talk about you," she reminded me. "So let's talk about you."

"Right. And my headstone will probably bear the same information, but I will know that I have expressed myself. My only fear is that my work would turn into some scholastic requirement where the books I wrote with a looming sickness in my head are autocratically shoved down the throats of our future children who will eventually loathe me and most likely never develop any keen interest in their adult life to willingly read my work."

She hummed over the line. It was a static hum, not to her fault.

"Have you tried opening up to friends and family?" she asked. "It could really help to have a support system."

"If I confide, they will say that I'm being miserable and depressing over trivial things that don't matter or, even worse, they will be overly sympathetic and compassionate without truly understanding. And because of this repugnant disease, oh, this awful, repugnant disease, I am driven back to writing. And if I or any other writer knew or were even acutely aware of what this disease was, they would put down their pencils, give away all their worldly possessions, and scour the world for the cure."

"I see."

"So now," I stated, "I give an alternative hypothetical: if I had the option of chopping off my arms or vaporizing certain faculties in my brain, anything that would render me unable to write or think in the way that I do, in exchange for the ability to gather around a dinner table and to truly enjoy myself without a single care about the words being said or about the things that are happening or about the people sitting next to me, I would have already signed my name to it."

"Have you taken any other approaches? How have you worked on yourself?"

"I try to spend time by myself and try to enjoy things simply for what they are."

"And how has that worked so far?"

"It's difficult. My mind cannot rationalize itself to know that a string of puffy cumulus clouds are just masses of water drops suspended in the air. They have to be more than that because there isn't enough for me. And I hate that I have this faculty in my head."

"Are you still working on yourself now?"

"Why work on yourself when there are so many distractions of freedom and comfort and pleasure to keep you broken? Why not just float in the excess like a discarded leaf in a body of water? It's quite inevitable too. Things that taste good and feel good and smell good swirl around you forever until you are completely distracted into your own death."

"But that isn't a good mentality to have. What can you do going forward?"

"Maybe I can write about something pleasant. Something beautiful. And I do try to enjoy the nice things. The trees, the flowers, the sunlight peeking through the clouds. But once I get comfortable, once I feel like I could really enjoy myself, the sickness erupts in my head like a siren. Maybe if I just had the ability to stare at something and recognize its existence, and nothing more than its existence, then maybe I could have that solace. But I have accepted the fact that I cannot just stare at a bed of flowers and find that solace. It doesn't work that way. But maybe I can look at a flower or a tree or a bug and realize it's importance is contained purely in its existence." I laughed a bit. "You know," I said, "from my balcony of dead plants, their leaves wilted and their stems rotten, I let a single flower, blooming with bright pink petals, hang off the side to let others know that there's still hope." And then I smiled in a sort of sardonic way. "But that's not a cure."

And as the light from the morning sun beams through my windowpane each day, I find myself further away. Drifting in the opposite direction toward nothingness. And the waves are pulling me further, my oars snapped at the shaft and rotten at the blade, my boat lacerated with cuts, letting the water seep in. Just let the wind keep blowing, I sometimes think to myself. For it will always blow in this direction and never in the other.

"It's not supposed to be a cure," she said. "It's supposed to keep you from falling."

There was a short silence over the phone.

"Do you think you'll be okay tonight?" she asked.

"I think," I said, thumping my fingers on my chest. "I think . . . I think I'm getting hungry." Then I felt a rush of excitement. "Have you ever had a pepperoni pizza from Piero's? The pizza shop off Hamilton Avenue?"

"No, I don't think I've ever been."

"The cheese is so gooey it hangs off your lips like string cheese. And the crust is always so fluffy and warm like cumulus clouds that were put in the microwave."

"I see."

"It's fantastic. Anytime you're in my city, definitely stop by. It's ten minutes out of Shilshine Bay. I'm going to call them and pick up a slice."

There was another brief silence over the phone.

Then the operator asked, "So will you be okay for tonight?"

"Yeah," I told her. "As long as they're open."

The Spider In The Stairwell

[Apartment]

Why sit down to write? Why are you checking the pantry again you ate five minutes ago. Only five minutes ago. Your stomach hurts. You ate too much again. A man coughing outside, I hope he's okay. I should water my dead plants again. Go back online. See what everyone from high school is doing. Jessica got engaged. They look happy. Pull your hair. I feel like I should be reading a book right now. This is a tormenting night. My back is aching. This couch is not comfy enough. Why did you get up again? You already ate, you're not hungry. You're not hungry, stop eating, you don't need to eat. Not right now. What time is it? Too early to go to bed. You're not even tired. But you're always tired. You have nothing to do. Wasting your life. You're dripping away. Check your phone. Where is it? There it is. The screen hurts my eyes. My eyes are in pain. In deep, fiery pain. Go to the doctor next week. Write a note to yourself about it. Organic romaine hearts, weird name for a food. Stop pulling your hair. Write ten pages. Just write ten pages. Jesus Christ how hard is it to write ten pages? Go to the gym tomorrow, but take the elevator. There's a spider in the stairwell.

[Gym]

Bangs and clangs and grunts and sweat, this place is disgustingly interesting. The air is salty and warm. I hear the air ventilation roaring. I don't think it's working. College student doing curls. A protruding Adam's apple. Cling clang bang. Grunting to lift the barbell. Things are discarded like they don't matter. I'm sweating a lot and haven't done anything. I don't want to finish this. I don't want to do this anymore. My arms are tearing themselves apart. I want to look better, but my arms are throbbing with pain. The lights are too bright. Why do they make them that bright? They're too fluorescent and they hurt to look at. They blinded me and now the walls are beginning to double. Pedal faster. My thighs are roaring in pain. Why did you make eye contact with her just leave or don't look there again. More clanging. I just ran into my friend and we traded handshakes. I hadn't talked to anyone for so long. I stumbled my words. I don't think he noticed. I hope he noticed. Then he would see that something was wrong. I am wrong. Wood pounded with basketballs protected behind glass walls. One quick game. No. One quick game. No. One quick game. No. One quick game. No. You're hurting. Okay, pick your hair. Keep lifting the weights and you'll still look like a tree branch. My toe is tingling with pain, I dropped a weight on it, why are you so clumsy you clumsy idiot. Clumsy, clumsy, idiotic. Why even come here if you can't even handle the equipment, everyone is looking at you like you're the biggest fool. That woman you made eye contact with thinks you're weak, and yes, weak you are. Weak you will always be. There's your story about a weak man who stays weak because he cannot fix himself or the world around him, destined to be subjugated by eternal sadness. There's your story. ~~Think~~ Ruminate about it. Think about it more. Does this work? There's your character. It's you.

[Cafe]

The music is too loud. Obnoxiously upbeat. A man in a ponytail ordering a pastry. A woman sitting across from me with a large book, spending more time on her phone than in between the pages. Who am I to judge? I do the very same. Who am I? I'm the one sitting here trying to spew. I just checked my phone, how hypocritical of me. This woman has a beautiful sundress on and looks to have no worries in the world. She will age well and find a nice man, I hope not one with a ponytail. My throat is dry and the water they gave me is lukewarm. If I sit here and write long enough, the cute barista in the black apron will come by and ask what I'm writing. And I'll tell her the next great American novel. And she'll be awestruck by my confidence. And the romance story will fly off the bookshelves at the kiosks in airport terminals. Beat, beat, beat. The music still thumps out of place. The metal chairs scrape the concrete floor. The baby outside is crying. Crying, crying, crying, and I don't know how the parents know what to do. Does anyone else come to cafes alone just to sit? Just to look around as I do? I see wooden benches and snake plants and discolored sofas. This isn't a normal cafe. . . . . . . Wow, you haven't pulled your hair yet. Pull your hair. Check your phone, you hypocrite. The girl with the large book left and was replaced by another woman with a phone but without a book. The air is heavy today, humid, tangy with the smell of the salt from the ocean. I thought if that's even the right way to describe it but solemn is a great word to use, put that in but look up what it means. Don't make eye contact with the heavy woman in the zebra dress. Don't make an animal joke either. My friend told me that yesterday was the latest sunset of the year, so every day that followed after would become darker and darker until I wake up in darkness and do the things I do to sustain myself and go to sleep in darkness. I used this word too many times it's ~~reductive~~ redundant. I want a shiny cup. Why did the man in the straw hat get a shiny cup, they gave me a plastic abomination. I want a shiny cup. Stop thinking about your past thoughts. You are endless. . . . . . . This woman in the summer dress has been tapping on her phone for the past ten minutes now. Pull your hair, no stop pulling your hair. Did you bring your comb? No? Start pulling. People have come in and out of the cafe. I got a message from a friend who finally responded after four days she was with friends at an off-grid cabin near a lake, how lovely of an experience that sounds. I wish I could have that if I could find enough friends I could spend that much time with consecutively, and I would fear that I would grow to hate them or that they would hate me. And I don't know why I have these thoughts, they just percolate to the surface without any warning, and there is no mitigation plan nor have I been able to create one. Pull your hair. Remember when your body wasn't in pain all the time? Remember when your mind was blissful and only concerned with what its eyes could see? Remember when you traveled to celebrate the holidays with your family? I hope I never have to celebrate my birthday again. My eyes are starting to water and I need to leave.

[Town Square]

What to write? Write. Write. Write. Girl wearing black shorts, ripped. Looks like they don't fit. A baby in a huggy seat. That's not the name for it, I'm sure. But it sounds proper. There's too many people here. I remember when there weren't so many. I thought the plague would fix that. It only exacerbated it. Too many people. Rent has gone up. The sidewalk is noticeably dirtier. I hate all these people enjoying themselves. That girl looks like a past partner of mine. She's going to the market with another guy. His arms larger than mine. I see a guy wearing a backpack from one of those big tech companies. I wonder what his pay is. His benefits. I also wonder . . . no. Such stupid thoughts. Clear them out. A coffee shop standing next to a pub. The morning and evening addictions, respectively. I wonder how many people are at the farmer's market across the street? Maybe two hundred? How large of a tsunami would it take to wipe them out? But then it would hit my apartment. My home would be underwater. And it would water my dead plants. Look at all these people with their friends enjoying a sunny Sunday morning. Here I am fighting through the infection. The sunlight is poking through the clouds and it will burn my forehead. Just write. Stop worrying about what it should sound like. It sounds like how it sounds. You're trying to self-edit. Stop it. Stop it. Corgis are shithole animals. One bit me a few months back. Pull your hair. This girl playfully shaking her head while sipping an iced coffee pisses me off. Her skin is too smooth. A man is screaming shut the fuck up to nobody. Why not put him through a woodchipper? Actually, he needs proper shelter and rehabilitation. I hope he comes over to me, tries to grab my computer and snap it in half. People are paying eighteen dollars for sunflowers across the street. Why do people wait in lines? It must be the majority of our life waiting in lines. Physical lines and non-physical. Those few moments before a meeting when you're just killing time. As if time could be killed. As if you could pull a knife and tear a hole through it like fabric, a hole big enough for you to step through it and into a different time. On hold with the bank. . . . . . . Everyone who was sitting near me had left. Why shoppe over shop? The same word. Shoppe lets you overcharge. Pull your hair. I like pink hair. Like bubblegum. More women should have pink hair.

Men should have blue hair. Cars keep zooming by. This town used to have so few people. Why is it so loud? Why is there construction? Why are there cars with loud exhausts? Why are there people who live here who look like they've never lived here? . . . . . . This is a cute couple. The woman is beautiful, mature, and properly socialized my god, I can never have someone like that, it requires a sort of peacefulness, stability, and she would want to go to dinner parties and happy hours and weddings of distant friends and I don't do well at any of those places, oh yes, write about that! A starving, tortured protagonist yearning for love. But it can't be you but it will always have a piece of me. . . . . . . The girl who was sitting two seats away from me left. I don't have anyone coming to meet me. How I wish there was some sort of community left in this town. How I wish I could just sit at one of the local cafes and see friends, people I know, walk by and have a small chat. . . . . . . A woman with sleeve tattoos, how regrettable! Do they maintain the shrubs in the town square? So many couples have passed me by. They look idyllic, happy. They must go home and shout at each other, throw ceramic dishes at each other. Nobody is always like that. Do you think someone will come up to me, right now, and strike some sort of pleasant conversation with me?

I think not. We're too scared of each other. I don't remember the last time I had talked to a stranger unless they were serving me something. And what a sad, un-reciprocal relationship we have with strangers. I hate that I'm going to have to edit all this vomit. I hate that this couple, walking past me, is young and without pain. I think they saw the envy in my eyes. Pick your hair. . . . . . . A man with thin legs like scissor blades. Two older friends meet at the corner of the street and exchange smiles. Have you smiled today? Smile. Feel the muscles move around in your face. No, really smile. More arm tattoos like Native American war paint. This isn't art. Stop picking your hair. A little girl in electric bolt pajamas running as fast as she can. Maybe I need a child so I can care about something other than myself. The cars keep roaring by. And the town was just about close to sounding quaint. A man with a feather in his hat just called a woman holding her man's hand beautiful. How many thoughts have I had so far since I sat down? Why are my eyes watery? How many people still have families? How many people are miserably alone? Are these friends walking together really friends? And there's a man, overweight, dressed in ragged clothing, limping with each step, with a jubilant smile on his face. . . . . . . The pills aren't kicking in yet. They will soon.

My back still hurts. Too many people pulling out their phones. We are already cyborgs. A little girl is painting nails on a digital tablet. Will her memories be as rich as mine when I was her age? Will she become dissociative? Will she not be able to distinguish reality from the delusions? Aleko sounds like a city in the Middle East. A street performer is playing Let It Be on the electric guitar. I want to go over and give him some money but I don't see him. I only hear the sound carrying over the air. I remember hearing that song when I was a child. My mind is a time capsule. . . . . I have some good memories, but I have to pull very deep inside of me to grab them. I haven't made any more of them in the past few years. It even pains me to recollect any sort of fondness in that time period. And I don't know why these are the thoughts that flurry in my head when I'm sitting here surrounded by happy, jovial people buying local produce and flowers on such a warm and sunny Sunday morning. I don't know why I think this way, I don't know why, I don't know why. Everything here is beautiful, can't you see you fool! But my eyes refuse to see. I cannot see things. I cannot see, why can I not see? You're as deep as a puddle. Go home, it's time to go home. Away from here. This was enough for today. Go home, but when you get there, take the elevator. There's a spider in the stairwell.

[Dinner]

The plates are too loud. The clanging of silverware hurts my ears. Too many people are chatting and I can't follow. I feel like an idiot. You forgot deodorant. People are probably looking at the missing chunk of hair on my scalp. It makes my chest tighten. Someone is sitting on my chest and I'm yelling at them to get up, but they won't. They are heavy like cinder blocks. Ciner, ciner, sinder. Look at other people. Why? I should have dressed better. Andrew is wearing a blazer at a sushi restaurant. I need deodorant. One of the girls said she loves late night talk shows. Smile, smirk, take a sip of water. Another sip. Don't say anything. Another sip. This is how you engage. Talk to Sarah. Say something nice or cute. Don't just stare at her. Ten, nine, eight, seven . . . are you a child? Why are your hands shaking, why is your body vibrating, are you sick, you are so afraid of everything. I shouldn't have asked about her work, I knew she didn't like talking about that, why does she hate me, my god she hates me. Nobody is talking to me. Nobody is asking me questions. Nobody cares about what I have to say. If I got up and left right now would anything change, no it wouldn't, I don't matter to this conversation, I don't know why I even get invited, I don't contribute anything, I might as well be that painting of a bonsai tree on the wall. Why can't you just enjoy the conversation and listen with your ears, someone might say something interesting. And something interesting could be useful to you. But everything I hear is awful, loud sharp sounds of shrapnel exploding in my ears. Light the sticks of dynamite and blow out the canals. Nobody has looked at me in five minutes. I haven't spoken in five minutes. The food came. Thank god the food came. Just eat your food. That's a good reason why you aren't talking. You're eating. They'll understand that. Just eat. Eat. Eat. Eat. Eat. Eat your food and shut up. They won't invite me again I'm sure. This was a social litmus test that I tremendously failed. The cinder blocks are heavier, why are they heavier, it doesn't make sense, please just let me be here, I don't have much more of this left. Why are you here? Go to the bathroom for a while and sit fully clothed in the stall. Long enough for them to worry. Or will they even worry? They will. I think they will, I hope they will. Talk to yourself closed in by the echoed walls, the marble tiles vibrating your words back to you. Come back and tell them that you're sick and that you need to go home. Go home, go home. You want to be home. You want to be there. You want to be alone. It's easier. This is too hard. Go home now.

[Apartment]

Now you're back here. Good job. You're back alone now. Write. Write. Watch TV. Count the little bumps on the wall. What to do now. I don't know. Just keep writing and that's all. Pull your hair. My plants are brown. My skin feels hot, pinpricks of pain on my scalp. I should be reading a book. I should call a friend. I don't want to. I should. I don't want to. Stop shattering the perceptions people have of you. Shut it off, shut it off. Keep writing. Don't stop. My stomach hurts now, but I want to eat. The ice cubes crackling in my glass of water. Stop pulling your hair. Pull your fucking hair. Plunge yourself into oblivion. The walls are keeping me in. Now I'm here by myself and it's cold. And I'm stuck with my thoughts, they're so ghastly. Why do you keep checking your phone as if your friends are going to care where you are or what you're doing or how you're feeling, stop checking and start living, but I cannot do that. Pull your hair right now. My back is starting to flare up. My eyes hurt too much to watch the television. My brain is too fried to read the words on a page. I thought I was able to understand everything about me with my last book. I thought I was, and oh how wrong I was, I was so wrong because I just opened the box, that box with three locks, locked so tight it was begging me not to open it, but I knew once I shattered it that I could not put it back together. Put yourself back together, put yourself back together, put yourself back together. Why am I wearing a straitjacket? I'm not. Then why does it feel like I am? Why are all my limbs tightened, wound up, and mummified? I am going crazy. . . . . . . I know people talk. And what would they say about me? Did you hear about Sam? He's all fucked up in the head now! He doesn't post pictures of himself having fun with friends with platitudinous captions, he doesn't go to fun parties, he doesn't see his friends too much, he doesn't do what everyone else who I think is stable does, and with my limited logic and reasoning skills, I can deduce that he is all fucked in the head! And no I haven't had any tactical human contact with him, I don't need to! I read his work, actually, a friend told me about his work, and I came to my conclusion from that. . . . . . . And my blood starts to heat with rage, and the sadness and melancholy turn to spite and contaminated anger. You need to calm yourself now. Calm yourself. Take deep breaths. This doesn't help. You're not helping yourself. This isn't working. Stop this, please. And why should I calm myself just to be here alone? Why would I do that? I'm alone. . . . . . . Maybe I should shroud myself in the darkness. Curl it over me like a thick blanket. How long would it take for people to care? How long before people got concerned about me? Or would the thought not even cross their minds? Is it sad that I derive a bit of pleasure from their worry? Is it terrifying that people know this about me? Why do I fantasize about the colors of the flowers on my memorial wreath? I don't think so because I think there are others who are too scared to admit they feel the same, but that doesn't make me any better and it doesn't make me any happier. And my head is steaming hot and I need to leave my room before I have an urge to break something. People understand you. Nobody understands you. Why does my body feel so hot? Scalding to the touch. Why does that feel like that? Is there something wrong? I'm not sure. Indigo, Indigo, Indigo. Beat, beat, beat, feel your heartbeat. Thumping and thumping, why is it like this, I don't know. Do you feel it? Feel it. Feel it now. Feel everything right now. Do it now. Do it right now. It's a lot. It's too much. I feel hotter. Get out right now. Just step outside. Use your feet. Those cold feet. Use them. Step outside. Go outside. Get out of your room. Get out now. Now. Now. Do it. Get out right now.

[Stairwell]

These carpeted steps need to be cleaned. Dirty. Too dirty. They feel too shaggy on my bare feet. The lights are too bright. Especially in the darkness. My heart is calm now. My chest feels okay. But am I okay? It's too late to be up right now. Everyone is asleep. Sound asleep and dreaming beautiful dreams. I can't remember my dreams. Not any recently. What was my last dream, I don't know. Just walk down the stairwell. Feel your feet on the old, shaggy carpet. Stop thinking. Stop it. Hold on. Breathe. Relax . . . .
. . . . What do you feel? . . . .
. . . . What do you see? . . . .
. . . .
. . . . Ah, I see you now . . . I finally see you now . . . I always try to pass you by or take the elevator, but I always have some urge to look at you. That one time when I was carrying four bags of groceries, I

ran past you and almost sprained my ankle, how funny! How funny that would have been. Look at you taunting me with your looks. You love that top right corner near the faint lightbulb. You love to let your spindly legs hang down like needles suspended in air. You love to look like such an ugly, hideous pest. How can you expect anyone to not want to kill you, that's absurd! Do you even have a purpose? Why do you exist? To make sure there aren't too many insects? Never mind that. It doesn't matter. I would be lying if I said I wouldn't have grabbed a shoe from my apartment and bashed you against the wall and splattered your guts everywhere, but I didn't because I'm not sure, and I just registered your hideousness in my head, and that was enough for me and enough for you, and I assumed that you would eventually move or be killed by someone else, but you didn't. I didn't want to kill you, it wasn't my responsibility! You grew twice in size and got twice as ugly. You should be dead by morning. Someone will see how big and plump you've gotten and will grab that thick Sunday newspaper that will get delivered tomorrow. Look at you now. So ugly to look at. And you just hang there unaware of how gross you look to us. Look at me looking at you . . . Hanging there by yourself . . . But look at you . . . look at you . . . I'm not sure what to think . . . . It's not your fault . . . . you are hideous . . . . sore to look at . . . . that's not your fault . . . . you just look like that . . . . you are existing . . . . just as I am existing . . . . And nothing more . . . . And that's you . . . .

. . . . You exist . . . .
. . . .
. . . .
. . . .

The Tree In The Town Square

If you didn't stop to look, you would never be able to see it. And seeing things can be quite difficult when one lives such a fruitful life. And the townspeople lived very fruitful lives.

The town itself was a small modish waterfront nestled near an inlet to one of the great oceans. Near the bay, boats with tall masts piercing into the sky filled the harbor docks, and the occasional beat of wings from the seagulls catching fish would carry over the hills. In the old industrial parts of the town, with disregarded buildings plagued by rust and graffiti, you could hear the whirring of forklifts and cement trucks and chatter from the construction workers.

The town itself, as it's important to note, has an immense urgency for business. The men and women work in a wide variety of professions from manufacturing, transportation, finance, education, healthcare, and real estate. And when they are not consumed with business or trade during the weekdays, they are consumed with leisure and pleasure on the weekends. During the gloomy and insipid days in the winter, ones that usually came with a sky of grey clouds and a torrent of rain, people stayed in the home watching movies or cooking meals, and aside from their place of work, some would occasionally leave their home to see a film at the triplex movie theater or enjoy an Italian dinner at one of the restaurants on the main market street. But on a summer day like this, you can find many people sitting outside of cafes enjoying a lemon tea or a caramel croissant accompanied by the small talk of one's work or the town's weather or something they read in the local news. At night, the young and free-spirited with metal in their ears and nostrils wait in long lines outside for expensive spirits while the older tend to their children or work.

This summer day, however, was no different than any other. The cafes were filled with chatter, cyclists glided through intersections of humming cars and buses, and the clatter of shoes bustled through the town square—a large rectangular area with brick floors in the middle of town. The town square itself was less of a localized meeting point like Times Square in New York or the St. Peter's Square in Vatican City and more of an entry and exit point, like a bridge connecting two land masses severed by a strait. To get to certain places around the town, it was quicker to simply walk through the town square as opposed to around it. The square itself had two metal benches for anyone who wished to sit, but few ever did.

In the middle of the town square, accompanied by a small bronze plaque, stood a lone tree. Its branches stretched out to touch the sky. Its trunk was firm and gripped to the ground. Its leaves danced delicately with the rustling wind. Compared to the shrubbery and bushes and hedges that were scattered around the town square, the tree stood the tallest—if that mattered, of course.

And on this peculiar summer day, a man in a brown hat was walking through the town square as a shortcut to the Shilshine Saloon. He was dressed modestly in a suit and tie and carried a leather briefcase. As he made it halfway through the square, he noticed that his shoe was untied so he set his briefcase down and tied it into a neat bunny knot. As he got back up, briefcase back in hand, he looked over at the tree standing tall in the middle of the courtyard. He had noticed the tree before. He had walked through the town square as a shortcut many times to get to the saloon or the print center or the property management office where he worked, but he had never stopped to look at the tree. It was always in the corner of his eye in a passing glance. But as he looked more at the tree, he felt an unusual wave of emotion carry over his body. An inexplicable one at first. And one that had seamlessly taken over his body. He did not continue walking to the saloon. No, any thought of walking to the saloon had left his mind. Instead, he stood there and looked at the tree. The flurry of thoughts that had rampaged through slowly dissipated like a blanket of fog confronted by the daylight. His body, his muscles, had seemingly relaxed and felt weightless. He released his grasp of the leather briefcase. It dropped to the ground, and the man in the brown hat continued to look at the tree.

Some time had gone by, maybe an hour or two, and the man in the brown hat continued to look at the tree. People continued to walk through the town square as they normally did. Many passed by and stared for a moment, but didn't say a word. It was a peculiar thing to see someone stare at something for so long, but it was also a normal thing to ignore such people who commit such strange acts. The idyllic waterfront town had its small clumps of wanderers and vagabonds, many of whom were dirt poor and addicted to opioids. A cafe full of patrons would occasionally be greeted by the howling jeers of one of these people, and the appropriate action was to ignore them and hope they would turn their attention somewhere else. But the man in the brown hat did not act or look like one of these wanderers. He was not barking at people, yelling obscenities in their faces with the heat and saliva from his mouth, nor were his clothes

113

tattered and smelly. He stood calmly and peacefully, wearing a clean suit and tie, looking at the tree.

It was for this reason alone that four hours had passed before another man, the owner of a bakery across the street from the town square, had approached him.

"Excuse me, sir," he said to him in a concerning tone. But the man in the brown hat did not answer. Instead, he kept looking at the tree. The baker raised an eyebrow. There was nothing remarkable about the tree, he thought. Yes, he had seen it from time to time when he gathered the wooden chairs inside from the front patio in the evening, but it was just a tree like any other with leaves and branches and roots. This fact perplexed the baker and made him insistent on speaking to the man in the brown hat.

"Good sir, are you alright?" he asked. "Is everything okay with you?" Still, the man in the brown hat did not respond. The baker scratched his head.

"Should I call someone for you?" he prodded. Still, no response. The baker became even more perplexed than he was before.

"Do you need any food?" he asked. "I have some leftover ginger biscuits if you're hungry. My wife insists we keep making them but nobody ever buys them so most of them end up in the trash anyway."

The man in the brown hat said nothing and stood still, looking at the tree. The baker mimicked his posture and stared at the tree.

"Is there any reason why you're staring at this tree?" the baker asked, but as he assumed, did not get a response.

Then, a woman on an afternoon run approached.

"Is everything alright here?" the runner asked with a shortened breath.

"I'm not sure," the baker told her. "This man will not speak. He just stares at this tree."

"I noticed that, too," she remarked. "I saw him here earlier when I was picking up deli meats at the market." She turned to the man in the brown hat. "Sir, is everything alright with you?"

He still did not respond. The baker and the runner were both stumped.

"Why do you think he won't speak?" the baker asked the runner.

"I'm not sure," she replied. "Maybe he's hallucinating. Apparently, there's been an uptick in ayahuasca use around town. I read about it in the paper."

"I doubt it."

"I wouldn't count it out," the runner pointed out. "My son had a friend from school who took ayahuasca at a retreat and got lost in the woods for hours until a rescue team found him hugging a tree."

"He's not hugging a tree, he's just staring at it."

"I don't see what the difference is."

Then, another person approached. A man with effeminate long hair wrapped in a ponytail wearing wire-frame glasses.

"What's going on with this tree? Is a show about to start?"

"It's not the tree," the baker corrected. "It's this man. He's been staring at it for hours without saying a word or moving a muscle."

"Oh."

The runner flagged down a police officer who was on an evening stroll through the town plaza. The police officer noticed and walked over to the small group clustered around the man in the brown hat.

"What seems to be the problem?" the officer asked.

"We're not sure," the runner told him. "This man has been staring at this tree for hours."

"And he doesn't speak or move," the baker added.

The police officer looked at the man and indeed, he stood still while looking at the tree. The police officer scratched his head.

"Sir," he said, putting a meaty hand on his shoulder. "Are you alright? Can I call someone for you?"

He did not respond, and the police officer became just as confused as everyone else.

"Why is he staring at this tree?" the officer asked the group.

"We're not sure," the baker said.

"Maybe the tree is special," a strained female voice from behind said. The local fortune teller, an older woman with earrings made of amethyst, squeezed herself in the group. "It has been here even before the town square. My grandmother used to tell me that the construction workers had just built around it."

"Built around it?" the runner questioned.

"Exactly," the fortune teller hummed with a smile. "They felt a supernatural presence coming from the tree, so instead of chopping it down, they built the plaza around it."

Gradually, more and more people gathered around to see the spectacle of the man in the brown hat. A few businessmen and women leaving their offices had joined after noticing the crowd of people in the town plaza. Nearby construction workers still wearing their hardhats and reflective vests with splotches of dirt on their faces had joined as well. At least two dozen had now clumped together, chattering amongst themselves. The town square had never been filled with people like this before, and each of them tried to talk to him, but like the outcome with the baker, the runner, and the police officer, he did not respond.

"He's a sick man!" someone from the crowd shouted. "He needs to be taken to the sanatorium up near Briar Lake."

"He's not sick!" a man carrying a box of pizza from Piero's said. "He's just lonely and sad. Probably just looking for attention."

"No!" a woman wearing a blue beanie chirped. "He's not well! He needs help and love and care!"

"It's not the man who we should be concerned about," the fortune teller asserted to the crowd. "It's the tree, I tell you! There's a supernatural presence coming from the tree. My grandmother used to tell me that the construction workers—"

Shortly after, a local news van arrived. A reporter in a sharp suit holding a microphone stood near the man in the brown hat and spoke into the camera. The live report garnered even more of a crowd. Now people were willfully leaving their homes to congregate to the town plaza. Some families brought their kids so as not to leave them home alone. Even a few crab fishermen came all the way from the harbor after hearing about the man on the news. Some people went up to the tree to examine it. Others started imitating the man in the brown hat, staring at the tree, hoping they could see what he saw. But after a few persistent minutes, and many breaks in concentration from the noise of the crowd, they gave up. Even a few tried to go up to him, treating him like a feral animal, and shake him free, but a group of policemen had surrounded around him. With a crowd nearing a hundred, and the yammering and chattering erupting in the air, the man in the brown hat, through everything, still did not move and continued to look at the tree.

The mayor of the town had arrived in the town square, escorted by the chief of police, and was brought face to face with the man in the brown hat. He stroked the stubble on his chin and narrowed his eyes, studying him like some new exotic animal in an exhibit.

"It is interesting," he concluded, stepping out of the line of sight so the man could continue to look at the tree. "How long has he been here?"

"About seven hours, sir," the chief sternly replied.

The mayor decided to have this peculiar man examined by a local physician. The physician, who hastily came after hearing that he was needed by the mayor himself, conducted a thorough exam. He took his pulse, examined his blood pressure, shined a flashlight in his eyes—which still fixated at the tree—pressed a stethoscope against his chest and back, and stuck a glass rod of mercury in his mouth to register his temperature. All tests came back normal with no signs of any abnormalities in his medical health.

"He's a sick man!" a man from the crowd shouted. "He's all fucked-up in the head!"

"He's not sick!" the man carrying a box of pizza from Piero's said. "He's just lonely and sad. Probably just looking for attention."

"No!" The woman wearing a blue beanie chirped back. "He's not well! He needs help and love and care!"

A rush of distressed chatter arose from the crowd, much like one you would hear from a group of protesters or a disgruntled audience at a town hall meeting. Then, people started yelling, flailing their arms in the air, uncomfortable with not knowing what kind of plague was tormenting this man. A group of policemen, as well as the chief of police, tried to squash the distress, but their cries were too loud. The mayor, with the idea of quelling the outrage, waved his hands in the air.

"People! People!" he shouted as loud as he could. "Let us not resort to this kind of behavior. I have an idea of how to sort this whole thing out. Please stop this outrage!"

And the noise from the crowd slowly dissipated like a fine mist. This man could be on opioids or other drugs, as the mayor keenly knew about the uptick in ayahuasca use in the town, or he could have traumatic brain damage. Either of which could explain this strange behavior, he concluded. Dipping into the town's expenditure, the mayor had a pathologist and radiologist driven in from out of town to conduct these reports. A rapid toxicology report was to be conducted by the pathologist and an MRI was to be conducted by the radiologist. He even brought in an arborist (on the insistence of one loud and persistent fortune teller) to examine the tree, much of which was ignored.

The pathologist had the man in the brown hat sit in a chair to draw his blood. They brought the chair behind him and with the help of two nurses, slowly lowered him down into the seat. The pathologist put the IV into his forearm and sucked the blood out. The man in the brown hat still looked at the tree.

For the MRI, however, the mayor thought about having the police escort the man in the brown hat to the nearby hospital, but thought of the act as somewhat authoritarian (especially with re-election looming in the future).

The radiologist, however, informed the mayor that he could have a portable, but expensive, MRI machine brought to the town square to conduct the test. The mayor was hesitant at first, as he had never heard of a portable MRI, unaware that such technology existed, but the radiologist assured him that not only did it exist, but that the machine was just as accurate as a standard MRI. The mayor agreed, took a bit extra out of the town's expenditure, and the radiologist came with the portable MRI machine.

The blood was drawn, the portable machine whirred and beeped, covering the entire head, and samples from the tree's soil were taken. The crowd eagerly awaited the results. The chatter had re-emerged but at a considerably lower volume. They spoke about what the results would be. Some confidently assured themselves that he was on some sort of hallucinogenic drug, had taken too much and was now trapped in some psychedelic trance. Others believed that his brain had malfunctioned, rendering him completely unaware of his strange behavior. Others weren't sure what to believe, but they waited just as eagerly as everyone else, and through all this chatter, the man in the brown hat continued to stand still and look at the tree.

Finally, the results were back. The arborist found a healthy stem and root structure and the organic matter for the soil was natural. The crowd seemed unmoved by this conclusion, except for the fortune teller, who scoffed from the back but was heard by noone. The pathologist found no traces of methamphetamines or barbiturates or any kind of drugs in the man's blood, while the radiologist found no structural abnormalities or brain damage in his MRI. The crowd fell silent for a moment, and let out a collective and disappointed sigh. The mayor felt like a fool for wasting town expenses and the news team felt a shared stupidity for wasting their time with such a tepid and uninteresting story. They had all dispersed, and very quickly the town square had become barren as if it had been recently evacuated, and the man in the brown hat was once again alone, looking at the tree.

A gentle wind kicked up a few stray leaves and shuttered the branches. Then, he took cautious steps forward until he was close enough to see the veins of the leaves and the protruding knobs on the branches. A discolored leaf that curled at the tips hung by a thread until it was seemingly plucked off by the wind. It fell to the ground delicately until a gust of wind picked it up again and sent it gliding out of the town square. He looked back at the tree and saw a spider with spindly legs hanging down from one of the branches, spinning an intricate and silky web.

And in that moment, the man in the brown hat had seen the tree and had consciously understood that this tree was a tree and how beautiful it was. He felt overwhelmed by the beauty that naturally existed in the tree. It needed no additives or modifications. It simply existed. And with an intoxicated mind, he walked back to where he had stood all that time, picked up his leather briefcase, and walked out of the town square.

The Importance of the Review

Dear Prospective Reader,

If you have made it this far in the book, you either read the whole thing or decided to flip to the back first. Either way, I am appreciative of anyone that reads through the pages of any of my works.

In this short letter, I would like to request from you, my prospective reader, an honest review of this novel. While, yes, reviews on listing sites such as Amazon and GoodReads help with listing rank and credibility, I am more interested in reviews for a different reason.

The relationship I have with you right now, after reading this book, is unfortunately unidirectional. I had just spoken to you for hours, possibly days, without hearing anything from you. I don't know how you feel. I don't know what you like. I can't read your facial expressions, whether pleasant or horrified, and I can't understand your thoughts. The words I write in the pages that you can physically touch are words that I have to pull out from very deep inside of me to share. And while I know how I feel about all the words that I have written, I am incredibly interested in listening to the people who take the time to read them. With that being said, I highly encourage you to leave a review on whatever online site you prefer. I welcome all reviews, positive and negative, and if you do not want your name attached to your thoughts, you are more than welcome to post it anonymously. I only ask that your review is genuine and in good faith.

That is all request and I want to thank you again for reading, I can't wait to hear from you.

Until we meet again for the next story,
Sam Calvo

Be sure to read Sam Calvo's first novel,

My Isabel.

And so begins Sam's journey of self-reflection and understanding. Although, he does not know it yet.

Struggling to fix the pains in his life that have tormented him for years—from grappling with a false identity, being trapped and enveloped in isolation, and refining his tainted and damaged ideology— Sam embarks on a trip to ease his mind and visit someone special: a woman who helped raise him for the first 12 years of his life. His Second Mother.

When he arrives, however, the once thought relaxing trip turns into an introspective adventure enriched with new and compelling ideas as he is offered help from the person he least expected. As Sam soon finds himself in a heightened form of reflection, he might now be able to navigate the entropic nature of living and finally understand the painful aspects of his life that, like so many of us, are desperately trying to figure out.

My Isabel is a philosophical journey lightly garnished with ingredients of magical realism, tapping into aspects of passion, meaning, happiness, enlightenment, responsibility, community, love, ideology, uncertainty, and so much more.

Available for purchase online on Amazon, Walmart, and Barnes & Noble

About the Author

Sam Calvo is the author of the philosophical and magical realist novel, *My Isabel: A Story of Reflection and Understanding.* He grew up in Washington State and currently resides in Seattle.

If you would like to get in touch with Sam Calvo, please send an email to sam@samcalvo.com

Thank You To My Beta Readers

Elaine Hong

Aria Frey

Natacha Silva

Ana & Josie

Brendan Richards

I Apologize

To anyone who has met me, seen me, spoken to me, been my friend, been my partner, or been my peer anytime before exactly right now at this very moment, I apologize.

I must have done something wrong.

I must not have been raised right.

I should have thought of how that would make you feel.

I didn't mean to make you feel that way.

I was dumb, naive, stupid.

Things in my life weren't right.

I've been really busy lately.

I was taking some time for myself.

I was being inconsiderate.

I shouldn't have said that.

I shouldn't have done that.

I should have said that.

I should have done that.

I should have said this sooner.

I should have said all of this sooner.

But sooner became later.

And later is now too late.

I'm sorry it's so late.

Made in the USA
Coppell, TX
09 October 2021